IF YOU CAN'T MISBEHAVE, THEN DON'T BEHAVE AT ALL (THE JOURNEY ENDS)

Harvey Price

Publisher: Harvey L. Price Jr.
Madras, Oregon

ISBN: 978-0-9819220-7-2

Library of Congress Control Number: 2011902748

Front cover: Homestead cabin, Culver, Oregon. Photo taken by author- 2010.

Back cover: Greg. Photo courtesy of The Daily World, Aberdeen, Washington/Macleon Pappidas.

Printed by Minuteman Press, Olympia, Washington and bound by Phil's Bindery, Seattle, Washington.

FOR

ALL THE HEROES WHO DEFEND, WHO DARE, AND
WHO HONORABLY AND NOBLY LIVE LIVES WITH
GRACE AND GOODNESS

AND TO THE WAGONERS WHO HAVE ATTEMPTED
TO SHOW US HOW

Also Written By Harvey Price

THE LAST ARK

SPEAK!

FETCH! (THE JOURNEY CONTINUES)

THE RETRIEVER

DON'T ROCK… THE BOAT!

ACCREDITATION TIME

DREAMMARE

ACKNOWLEDGEMENT

The study of behavior... whether it be good, wondrous, brave, questionable, bad or evil is as old as humanity's journey from its earliest beginnings. It is the ultimate factor as to whether we succeed as a civilization to curb our passions and willfulness and become custodians of goodness. The "doomsday" clock for an atomic Armageddon would almost seem to have been replaced by a "misbehavior" clock. And the midnight hour may be getting closer at hand. It is the Wagoners' hope throughout the story that follows that they may help reduce the potential chiming of that midnight hour. It is to both members of this little clan and to others of you out there who toil daily to bring forth and protect that goodness in our everyday lives... everywhere... that this story acknowledges and honors. You are the true heroes.

FOREWORD

For anyone who reads any of my books, the theme of 'starting over' will soon become evident. It was not something I intended to have played such a prominent role in these various stories. It just happened. But maybe it is a universal theme; one that not only fills the pages of literature, but the days of our lives. Certainly, I qualify for someone who has done far more of this that others should or would want to. But there should be no shame in that. Recognizing our fallible human nature and asking... indeed, praying for guidance and hope, are the cornerstones of avoiding and preventing the steep decline into unacceptable behavior. Starting over is the backbone of that process. And likewise, so is the lifelong journey of finding wisdom and becoming the hero's that are so desperately needed in these fitful times. So, may all your days begin and end with a sense of completing, step-by-step, the starting over you have possibly undertaken. The Wagoners each understand and salute you for doing so. As do I.

APPENDIX

Here is the test of wisdom,
Wisdom is not finally tested in schools,
Wisdom cannot be pass'd from one having it to another not having it,
Wisdom is of the soul, is not susceptible of proof, is its own proof,
Applies to all stages and objects and qualities and is content,
Is the certainty of the reality and immortality of things, and the excellence of things;
Something there is in the float of the sight of things that provokes it out of the soul.

> -Taken from 'Song of the
> Open Road', as incorporated
> in Walt Whitman's epic
> poem, "Leaves of Grass"

The Individuals Mentioned in "If You Can't Misbehave, Then Don't Behave At All" (The Journey Ends)

Name	Species	Function	Place of Origin
Greg*	dog	Sage	Atlantic City
Flo*	dog	Being Faithful	Atlantic City
Wally*	child	Boy Wizard	Atlantic City
Bernie*	child	Girl Herald	Atlantic City
Sophie*	adult	Nurturer	Atlantic City
Frank*	adult	Organizer	Atlantic City
Jennifer*	cat	Rebuilder	Atlantic City
Rita*	bird	Rebuilder	Atlantic City
Capt. Phil Shriver	adult	Commander	Polar Wind
Stella Shriver	adult	Facilitator	Willa's farm
Willa	?	Guardian	Anteverse
Walt*	?	Vanguard**	Anteverse
Happy *(aka Sparkie)*	dog	to be duped	Polar Wind
Goodie	dog	The Duper	unknown
Jimmy	adult	Driver	Willa's farm
Diane	adult	Survivor	Willa's farm
Lilyanne	kid	Greg's co-Messenger and one of Wally's Special Envoys.	Chico
You, the reader		The Audience	

*The original Wagoners
** In the Anteverse a Vanguard is also a Wizard.

PROLOGUE

ONE: BERNIE'S LAMENT

Again and again I have had to face and now finally recognize that what you hope for, eagerly anticipate happening or joyfully expect should be some outcome will not necessarily ever occur. It's as if you are given fleeting visions of a promising future, blessed and sheltered by a loving and benevolent Creator and unexpectedly become altered by someone gifted with remarkable powers to alter the worldly status quo, only to be frustrated over and over by the one variable that none of us could permanently change for the common good.

It is only at the insistent urging and a promise to one of my dearest companions, one who along with Flo, saved my brother and I that day in Atlantic City, that I am following up with completing this record of our time together. And while it's true that my duties as a Herald would imply that I should, by all rights, do so, I am not by nature or vocational calling a scribe. Nor do I intend to proceed with the Herald duties beyond this present effort.

Admitting this, you should not expect what I report to be especially entertaining.

However, any subsequent reader of this record will still be treated to a major portion of it being originally documented by our usual and faithful chronicler... Greg. His dedication to this task meant I have had to pour over his dictated notes, some of which even Willa had written down for me to use. And it has taken me many months to piece them all together in chronological order. At every point in this effort, I have worked to maintain both the content and spirit of what Greg was trying to say. And you will note that his personal impressions or thoughts are always highlighted by my using an *italic script*. Any omission or awkwardness in the final draft is solely my fault. You will not find my own personal thoughts until the end of this report.

For now, I should leave the details of the Wagoners final journey and days together in his own words. My own last obligation to you will be to reveal what influenced and led to its final outcome.

A NEEDED BREATHER

TWO: THE BIRTHDAY PARTY

Everyone or everything, whether they be plants, invertebrate animals, fish or amphibians, reptiles, birds or mammals...edible or not, it now seems can speak. It's like, between Walt and Wally's vast, worldwide transformations, there are arguments, threats, counter threats or sometimes even civil conversations taking place everywhere... and all at once. They gave many who were mute the ability to speak, a most powerful main course. And it has caused a ravenous hunger to communicate and explore... all at once. But I'm already becoming more and more aware that they failed to include a few appetite suppressors... like a dash of reasonableness, a pinch of thoughtfulness and a heaping side dish of an unknown, something else that eludes me, and yet I knew it must be included to curb this pent-up need to gorge themselves.

And I was more and more aware of this that same day we rode the New York City subway down to Penn Station from the United Nations Building. Even then, the impact of what they had done and the need for some kind of follow up was becoming evident.   But each of us Wagoners needed rest... and lots of it. We needed to get back to Willa's as soon as possible. Our around the world cruise had taken an emotional and physical toll on each of us.   Maybe now the world could meet and work out its troubles while we caught up on some sleep.   At least I hoped so.

As we rode in that subway car to Pennsylvania Station to catch our train for Chicago and then transfer to the one that whizzes you across the northern tier states to Seattle, I couldn't help but notice that most of the dogs I saw were still on a leash. And that was not working out well. Most of them were yelling at the people holding the other end of their tethers. Barking and growling appeared to have become passé since our road trip across the country.   And those who did relinquish using a leash appeared to have lost complete control of their used-to-be "pets".

If us dogs were able to stand on our two hind legs and put our front paws on our waist (something we obviously don't have), I'm sure most of them would have assumed that pose and would be doing so as they responded to their "owners" demands and protests. It was clear to me at this early stage that giving the ability to speak to most of God's creatures was still a work in progress.

And rather than the few cats that I noticed on our particular subway car just lying quietly on the lap of their "significant other", they were also shouting at the nearby dogs who seemed to be gawking or ogling them. Countless times I heard them hiss objections at being stared at. Outbursts were easily overheard, ones like "Hey! You hairy doormat... got a problem?"; "Yo! Fleabag! You're drooling... Typical. How nice"; or "You! Dog's Breath! You're panting so hard we'll soon have to exterminate or evacuate... eyes right and CLOSE YOUR MOUTH!"

It was all so unnerving, particularly when our group had hardly any time to recover from our Polar Wind trip. In fact, we all just huddled together after my initial barking outburst. I cuddled up at Sophie's feet, and Flo lay next to me. We just stared at the other dogs and cats onboard that subway car. They all seemed to look at me as if barking was probably all I could still do. It was a look that said I should be admitted into some institution for the severely mentally handicapped without delay. How little did they actually know. I could have just as easily signaled to Wally and motioned for him to transform them briefly into mutant toads and then see how they reacted. Instead, I just sighed, glanced over at my best buddy, Flo, and hoped we'd be getting off at Penn Station soon.

We arrived at Penn Station at 4: 45 p.m. and were met by a tidal wave of humanity and a sizable portion of its domesticated wildlife. Never, even in my more carefree days in Atlantic City, did I ever see so many and so much of everything in one place! It was like when we were back in Cairo, with its teeming streets. At that moment I felt as if all those same streets had somehow been stuffed inside this underground train station. I wanted to jump up into Sophie's arms and have her carry me... all twenty-nine, hairy pounds of me.

Rita hopped up on Flo's wide back and clung on tightly with her claws fully extended. Jennifer, ever-clever as always, managed to plead... or more accurately, whine enough, and got Bernie to pick her up and carried her. And as she and Bernie passed by me, she looked down at me at

5

one point and just smiled that 'I'm so special; and, even after all that we've done, you're still just a dog', look at me.

Maybe humans have their own crosses to bear, like making the bed, raising the lid on the toilet seat, sorting socks, keeping track of their car keys; BUT dogs have cats. Don't even try to bother me with your trivial complaints.

Through his usual magical transformations and manipulations, that I had now become uncommonly accustomed to, Wally had somehow arranged for us to have reservations on the next train to Chicago. My suspicion was that he did this when we were still at Willa's, because he also, in addition, had arranged for us to have the largest sleeper compartment on the train going from Chicago to Seattle. However, he was only able to secure coach accommodations for our trip from Penn Station to Chicago. How little did he know what riding in a coach would entail and what the consequences of it would be.

Anyway, we had just enough time to wiggle our way through Penn Station to the platform where our train was already rumbling excitedly, as if anxious to be on its way. It was due to depart at 5:15 p.m. And if anything, the onrush of people (and an odd assortment of mammals and birds) only intensified as we approached our particular car.

I actually wondered if there had been a call to immediately evacuate the building and that was why everyone and "everything" (if I can be so casual to use such a term for myself and any others with similar amounts of body hair, or fur and feathers) were now rushing madly into our one, waiting car.

So out of fright and desperation, I let out a snarling roar-of-a-bark.

Instantaneously, Sophie spun around and hissed at

me, "Gregory!! Stop That This Instant!!!"

Now, then, hearing her address me for the very first time as "Gregory" got my fullest attention. I thought only Popes, movie stars or notable comedians had that name. I swear my ears and stubby tail became fully erect at that very instant... and I became motionless and speechless.... or bark-less at her feet.

Looking up at her, with no small amount of remorse at having disappointed my most favorite person ANYWHERE and even with the mounting flood of boarders backing up behind us, I halted the boarding of everyone and muttered, "Sorry, Sophie. I'm getting the jitters. I've never been on a train before, and if it's going to be as crowded inside here as it is on this platform, I'd rather travel anyway else, even if it's by pulling that stupid wagon with Wally in it."

"Well, have you thought that through enough to think he might not be so taken by the idea... him, as well as the rest of us. Peddling across America was definitely not my dream vacation... along with all that business with Walt, Po and those terrible Emissaries. At least once we are onboard this train, we have assigned seats; and they don't allow passengers to travel standing in the aisles, like was done on the subway train we just rushed off to get here. So, CALM DOWN! You're getting to be a real pill, Greg!"

Now that struck home: Sophie scolding me. It was at that moment I decided that all of us needed some time out. Rescuing creatures, trees and the inhabitants of this planet had taken its toll. Never... EVER... did I expect Sophie, of all people, to react so... even to me. It was a sign for sure. And I decided then and there, just before making the climb up onto the step-stool, which led to the first steps of the car's doorway entrance, that I would try and be as pleasant and unflappable as was possible... despite my genetic predisposition to do just the opposite when under stress. We were all frayed. It was simply that I was the loosest cannon of the bunch. It was bound to be me who would explode first. We couldn't get to Willa's fast enough for a long retreat. Our missions of magic and mercy were over. The peoples and other speaking flora and fauna everywhere would have to adapt without us... or so I hoped.

Resolute with those thoughts, I jumped up onto the final step and wiggled my way into our designated coach. And as panic was replaced with relief, I hurriedly scurried behind Sophie to the seats she and Frank were assigned. Bernie and Wally were to be seated immediately in front of them. In other words, each set of seats faced one another.

This arrangement seemed rather odd to me, after having just flown out to New York City from Seattle in which the seats were positioned back-to-back. That seemed more private somehow. This arrangement meant you stood a better chance of accidentally kicking one another... provided you had long enough legs.

As it turned out, the next pair of seats, which also faced each other, was for Flo, Jennifer, Rita and myself. And as you probably already guessed, our particular assignment was for Jennifer and Rita to sit together and Flo and I were to sit directly across from them.

Realizing this, I couldn't help but be less than thrilled that I had been given the opportunity to face Jennifer, who alternates on rare occasions with being a close confidant or, at moments like these, with potentially being the 'Lordess of the Universe'. I secretly wondered if it would be possible to hold my breath as we traveled all the way across America…

And soon enough everyone in our assigned car settled into their designated seats, and just like Sophie had promised me, everyone and everything became quiet and calm. There was almost an air of expectancy as the long train prepared to launch… or whatever they say when trains gear up and begin to move.

And knowing that I didn't have to pull anything like that blasted wagon this time around, I became quite euphoric.

In fact, I began jumping up and down on the seat next to Flo.

"FOR THE LOVE OF PETE! CAN'T YOU JUST SIT STILL FOR ONCE!! Rita squawked, with an accompanying shriek that only a severely wounded cockatoo could screech out. It blasted your eardrums and almost made me sick at my stomach.

And because I had never heard that expression before, I thought she was directing it towards someone across the aisle, sitting behind her; a guy she somehow knew who was named, "Pete". But then, after that plausible assumption, I next happened to notice that she was looking straight at me. I realized then that for some reason, she had called me "Pete". That, alone, convinced me she had been spending too much time around Jennifer.

That was it. I couldn't wait to get out of New York City. And if we didn't hurry, I sensed every one of the Wagoners was eventually going to celebrate an 'off-to-the-pound-party' for me. Never mind that for years and for thousands of miles I had carried magical potions in the tip of my ever-itching tail for Wally or that I could be Bernie's mouthpiece for alerting audiences scattered across the world that it was past time for them to help bail out and tow humanity's often floundering or near-sinking ship, it was my additional responsibility to walk, sit, stand patiently and to do so with impeccable reserve. But dear reader, and to all those others who can't, let me be very clear: that just isn't going to happen... at least not in my lifetime.

In hopes of seeking some kind of reprieve, I glanced nervously over at Wally, sitting across the aisle from me and who had not said one word... that I knew of... since our leaving the United Nations Building. Even he was silent as I was being reprimanded. MY BEST BUDDY! He just continued looking out the window.

I wanted to shout, "Hey YOU! Yeah, YOU, sitting over there with that silly cap on your head with the slowly revolving propeller on the top... REMEMBER ME? I NEED SOME SUPPORT OVER HERE! I know you must be really tired from rescuing the world from certain destruction, but there are still matters needing your immediate attention: ME... for instance."

But he never even turned his head toward me. Even Flo sat unmoved and silent beside me.

I felt like I was back on Howard's porch again in Atlantic City; like nothing over this last year or so had ever happened. And suddenly I sensed that this must be what someone feels when they are at a major hump or transition time in their lives. Too often, it little matters what you have attempted or accomplished in your life to that point, the public, those who are total strangers and those who were your closest confidants are too busy with their own lives to spend time acknowledging or recognizing you. If you believe you've done your job well, be satisfied and content. That's your reward. But if you continue to call attention to

yourself, you will become a clown or worse, a nuisance...
an irritating distraction in their own lives, and even worse,
a source of conflict as they attempt to cope with their own
personal challenges. That thought really depressed me.
And I sincerely wanted to find a seat by the window and
just stare out of it.

And that is when I caught the eye of a conductor beginning to pass through our car. I decided there and then to ask him whether there was a place I could do just that: stare out the window. And when I did, his answer was to soon begin my having the most wonderful trip of anyone's lifetime. Why? Both this train and the other one we were to take out of Chicago had Lounge Cars.

Then just as soon as he told me that all of us felt a slight jolt; and as we glanced out the windows, we noticed that everyone and everything was either walking or running backwards or that we were actually moving forward ourselves. And despite the mounting objections of my cohorts around me, I still could not help myself and hollered, "LOOK AT THAT!! WE'RE MOVING! WE'RE GOING HOME!"

And to my surprise, Flo turned and smiled at me, nodding in full agreement; and Wally, who at some point had stood up in his seat, reached over and patted me on the top of my head and replied, "It's going to be ok. Come on, let's both go to the Lounge Car. I, too, am so relieved we are heading home to stay... at last."

And despite my penchant to avoid such behavior, never having been one to express myself in such a manner, for the first time in my life I got down off my seat, walked around the aisle, heaved up on my back legs, placing my front paws on the armrest of Wally's seat, and arched my head forward enough to give my dearest buddy in the whole world a warm, moist and heartfelt lick on his cheek and answered, "Yeah, let's do it."

For the remainder of the trip to Chicago, starting that late afternoon of April 25th, much of which is now mostly a blur, Wally and I sat or lay down in the Lounge Car seats, which faced the passing scenery. And as the trip got underway, our seats allowed us to look out on the Hudson River.

And anyone who has ever seen or read about our previous exploits knows how much I admire or actually almost worship rivers.

Come to think of it, if I was someone appointed to make totems or statues of deities, that job would have been easy for me. I would have said they were unnecessary. My incantations and prayers of supplication would have been to rivers. To me, they represent the mystery and wonder of life, even more so than those oceans we crossed over these last few months.

Rivers meander through the countryside like us talking folks do throughout our lives. Perhaps we like to think that we are on a straightaway course to eventual success, everlasting happiness or redemption, but upon closer examination, we will find out it just isn't so. Rivers begin their journey almost magically, often mysteriously hidden on a remote mountain side. Our own births are no less wondrous. And each river's capacity to absorb their feeder streamlets, creeks, runoff and occasional floods mirror our own daily experiences, which can be anything from unrecorded, casual, mildly noteworthy to life-altering. Rivers bring life into being and sustain it, just as we do. Most of all, however, even after all this is acknowledged, rivers tug at the desire and hope for immortality in each of us. They appear timeless in purpose and in beauty. And the Hudson River was no less so than any of the others I had crossed or seen in my travels. It becalmed me, as I sat there with Wally, my ever-trusting companion through that evening until the next day.

Upon our arrival in Chicago, Wally and I quickly made our way back to where the other Wagoners were seated. Only Flo had bothered to come forward during the night to check on whether we were ok. She had stayed with us for an hour or so while we watched the scattered, very isolated lights blinking in the distance, as we hurried through the farm country of Ohio and Indiana.

It was a totally different experience from the last time we drug those wagons through these two states. There was almost a disconnected feeling now, like we were out in the darkness of infinite space and looking out upon twinkling starlight. It was comforting on one hand, but on the other, it gave you the sensation of isolation and struggle.

Each light represented a family working feverishly to survive, even in this unwelcome blackness, which can offer neither light nor hope. It just is. It's the light that is special, and Wally and I knew it. And for some unknown reason, that time together for us signaled there was still more darkness ahead for us. This land was not healed, nor yet hardly healing. True, there were now more conversations, more participants in the discussions... all without the external evil of the Emissaries. But something disturbing was still ever-present. It was an enveloping blackness that could extinguish the small, fragile lights we saw, as we passed. But for us to provide anyone help, we first needed rest and lots of sleep.

And that brings me to the next train we were to catch. Our arrival in Chicago was preceded by our train passing slowly through its "South Side"... for miles and miles. I had never seen anything like that before.

It seemed like a world being kept apart and isolated. It appeared to have a large population, one which had been making repeated attempts at building homes, businesses, neighborhoods... a life. Sadly, these attempts only became stymied or frustrated by some higher power or authority or, more likely by some raw-boned, unofficially condoned but widely held bias-prone elite, to keep a portion of the population, and in this case, a very large portion, on the margin of society. Looming beyond were the skyscrapers and successful businesses which seemed to serve as a fortress wall to keep out those who lived in this expansive neighborhood. It reeked of poverty, lost opportunities and dashed dreams. And I knew straight away that whatever it was that perpetuated this large scale, desolated expanse of poverty needed to be exposed and somehow changed.

I didn't see anything like that elsewhere on our trip across this country when pulling our wagons. We intentionally dodged larger cities. And our recent flight into New York City and then leaving it by way of the Hudson River route, I was not made aware of such an expanse of purposeful isolation in that city. But I knew then and there I needed to talk to Wally and Bernie about all this once we got settled back at Willa's place. Maybe the core sources of evil had been purged by Walt and Po, along with Bernie and Wally, but there was still something wrong. Really wrong. And it confused me.

But these thoughts were soon forgotten as Wally and I heard the conductor announce our upcoming arrival at the Chicago terminal. All passengers were instructed to head immediately back to their assigned seats.

Once we got back to our fellow travelers, we were greeted with some telltale glances, particularly from Rita and Jennifer.

"Did you have a nice time in the Lounge Car?" Rita almost sneered.

"Yeah," Jennifer quickly added, "Nice of you to invite the rest of us to join you."

Luckily, it was Wally who answered their question and comment. If it had been me, it would have launched another round of squawks, hisses and barks.

"We just wanted an unimpeded view of the passing scenery," Wally quickly replied. "You should have joined us. There was plenty of room for everyone. Most everyone just came and went; nobody stayed very long, except for Greg and me. On our next leg of this trip, you both must join us when we make our way to the Lounge Car."

As usual, whether the soothing comments came from either Wally or Bernie, they would soon cool the mounting tension that might suddenly arise between us less-mannered furry and feathered folk. Like pouring cold water on a simmering pile of wood shavings, his remarks dampened their mounting resentment.

Rita then turned to Jennifer and said, "That's a great idea! Let's do it, Jen!"

I was left looking up at Wally in total disbelief. Why does nice always have to be at the expense of happiness and contentment? I couldn't help but wonder...

Anyway, we Wagoners soon piled out of our assigned car into the surge of everyone heading into the terminal. It was late afternoon, but our connecting train, The Empire Builder, wasn't scheduled to leave for Seattle until 8:30 p.m. Luckily, there was a special lounge area inside the terminal where people and folks like Flo and I could rest and get a snack while waiting for our train. It apparently was reserved for anyone having sleeper car arrangements or was a frequent traveler. Little did I know until then that we were in the former category. But I wanted to get a head start on sleeping, so I just curled up at Sophie's feet once she got settled and slept until she nudged me to get up and proceed to our next train's connection.

Now there were two events during this up-coming, cross-country train ride that probably deserve some detailed explanation. If nothing else, they will give anyone reading this earlier account some insight into our frame of mind and, more likely, the steely purposefulness we would need for the tragedies that were awaiting us.

It's often the inconsequential events in life that mark your pathway to the stars; or more likely in my case, your slippery slide into oblivion...

The first episode began almost immediately after we entered our designated sleeper car, which I had absolutely, no prior knowledge would be our good fortune.

When I was first told we'd be traveling in one, I thought it was just going to be something like my usual place to sleep, which would most often had been on a porch; various carpeted, tile or hardwood floors; or most recently, and luxuriously, on an old sofa at Willa's. Little did I realize that it could have been an actual six-foot long, three-foot wide BED! True, I probably would have had to share it with Flo, but that would have been ok with both of us as well. We canines stick together.

The complication arose when it was learned that it was to be in a VERY SMALL COMPARTMENT WITH BUNK BEDS, AND JENNIFER AND RITA WOULD

ALSO BE SLEEPING WITH US.   Compounding that arrangement was how and by whom it would be determined as to who had the top bunk. My suggestion, drawing on the old adage: 'Fair for One, Fair for All', was that all four of us should sleep on the bottom bed.   Initially, that most democratic idea was met with complete and total silence. That should have been my first clue as to what was coming next.

This awkward pause later reminded me, once again, that any legislative or diplomatic skills I had were quite rudimentary.   Most likely, this deficiency was due to a personal philosophy I had developed over time. Basically, it could be summarized easily as follows: 'To eventually satisfy everyone, you must first start with yourself'. And oddly enough, it did seem to be the norm I was noticing come from various centers of government, even after the end of the Emissaries' reign.   Sacrifice, loyalty and statesmanship were oftentimes a veneer or varnish brushed over one's self prior to getting into office. Once there, it was time to get down to the real business of governing: self-promotion and acquiring as quickly as possible the entire range of creature comforts that one so obviously deserved. And at that moment... for me, using that top bed did not fall into those first three, noble character traits. I may be covered with hair and speak slowly, but I still know a choice comfort zone when I see one.

It would be a strenuous effort for me to scramble, somehow, up onto that higher bed, given that there were no steps or a ladder. And I certainly couldn't do a six-foot, standing jump or even a running jump. Maybe if the train provided trampolines it might be possible or if the porters could lift me up there. But what about Flo? Lifting an 85 pound husky in that enclosed space, with her squirming nervously all the while, would be hopeless. As far as that goes, it would be rather simple for Rita and Jennifer to either scamper or fly up there, but neither apparently would have anything to do with it.

This noted; what happened next probably deserves some staging. The characters involved should already be familiar to you: Flo, Rita, Jennifer, myself, Sophie and Bernie. The scene included the lower bunk bed, which had already been nicely arranged by the train attendant; and the adjacent hallway, which was the main corridor for anyone passing into and out of our particular car. In short, it was the train's main thoroughfare. Two compartments had been reserved by Wally for this final leg of our trip home. One was ours, and the much larger and more spacious one was for Sophie, Frank, Bernie and Wally. It had its own restroom and multiple beds. It was an ensuite… of sorts… on wheels. Those four had already eagerly retired inside their compartment, which was designated as Compartment Eight, when 'conference time'… if I should be so liberal in the use of that term… for Compartment Nine's members of the animal kingdom began.

What had begun as a simple suggestion by me quickly morphed into a full-scale shout-fest. I believe it was Rita who first got Compartment Nine's 'over-my-featherless-immobile-carcass-you-will' discussion started with those now-infamous words: "Sheets, pillowcases, mints left on pillows and DOGS don't mix! Not on bottom bunk beds in trains… and not even on top bunk beds! Who knows which came first: floors or dogs? But they go together like horses and flies!"

Now, then, I could probably agree, to some extent, with some of her observation. It always seemed somewhat demeaning to me to see photo's of dogs sleeping on beds.

It was like we were caving in to some cultural trend that would ultimately weaken us or make us fluffy, like rag dolls or Teddy Bears. I mean a real dog has to have that musky odor of the wild and untamed, of having just happily and repeatedly rolled over a luckless, days-ago abandoned, dead fish on the bank of some rugged wilderness' onrushing river. And whoever came up with the idea of bathing us should have to grow multiple layers of thick, dog hair and then get plunged into icy, cold, sudsy water and see how mortifying that is. The few times that has happened to me I felt like all I needed afterward was for someone to tie a pink ribbon around my tail and put a girly bonnet on my head. I ask you, does the whole world have to be feminized? Deodorized and sanitized? So score one for Rita.

Rita's outburst was immediately followed with Jennifer exclaiming, in a tone that indicated that cats sleeping side-by side with dogs was easily comparable to sheep sharing sleeping bags with wolves, "ARE YOU CRAZY?!!", she yelled. "For one thing, that bed wouldn't hold all four of us. And to do so would mean we'd have to touch one another…" Saying this was immediately followed by a visible shudder.

And it was at this point that both Rita and Jennifer aroused the dormant but unwavering personality and never-before-yet-seen ire of Flo. It was a BIG mistake.

Ever since I first met, Flo that day we literally ran into each other on the streets of Atlantic City, to that last, delightful evening we spent on the New York City to Chicago train, I had never seen her angry. Her entire affect had always been one of pensive reserve or of a kind of untouchable melancholy for her ancestral home.

But not this night. From behind me, but in full view

of both Rita and Jennifer, I heard this roaring voice cry out, "QUIET!! BOTH OF YOU!!! We have experienced so much together, traveling for countless miles to exotic shores and hostile lands, all the while being part of almost indescribable transformations; and you still stoop to acting like this. It's as if what we have seen and done has had no impact, whatsoever, on either of you.

"Granted, Greg here has the uncanny ability to test our patience a bit, but each of us has learned that there is not one, hairy inch of guile anywhere on or in him. If he makes a suggestion, it is not for any other reason than to gather his friends around him and to celebrate. I honestly think he is so innocent and unaware that even in his sleep he is probably dreaming about how to help us all share good fortune and happy times together. He is the true definition of what it means to be a 'party animal'. The perfect lifestyle for him would be to own an immense hotel in Las Vegas. He'd set up shop inside its Lobby and greet everyone who came in with infectious enthusiasm and much tail wagging.

"But it's not with you two alone who I am beginning to sense the increase of inappropriate, even bazaar behavior and decision-making. My sense of smell, along with my perception of both the people and us critters has led me to believe that a general breakdown is occurring all around us. And in you two it is very unbecoming. So stop it! And apologize to Greg right now!"

And just as there was probably going to follow Flo's rather generous remarks about me an earth-rattling event in that compartment and along the adjacent, narrow hallway, Bernie and Wally came scampering out through their compartment doorway.

And right away, I sensed that we were not going to

escape Bernie's wrath nor possibly even Wally's wand or staff's unpredictable transformations. In about the next ten seconds I could envision myself jetting across the cosmos having been transformed into some kind of rather hairy, barking asteroid.

"What in heaven's name is going on here?" Bernie called out as she approached us.

"Yeah, that's what I'd say. And why can't you four get along?" Wally chimed in, as he was dangerously groping into his back pocket for that collapsible wand of his. "Is someone else bothering you?" he added, which I thought at the time was an overly generous inquiry, given our long-running history of disagreements with each other.

"YES!" Rita squawked. "It's Greg again! He's just impossible!! He seems to think all four of us can sleep on the lower bunk bed at the same time, and both Jennifer and I think it is very inappropriate for him to even suggest it. We're females after all. It just isn't proper."

Now that remark took me by surprise. Not since the formation of the Wagoners could I recall hearing a discussion or disagreement about someone's gender. I mean if you were to look at either of them, do you think you could have known right away that they were either male or female? I only assumed so when they told me their new names back in Atlantic City. For all I knew they could have even been fellows who just fancied a girl-type name when each of them decided to take one. It didn't matter to me who or what they were. But then there's that whole issue of being neutered... I'm not going there. That gets way too confusing. I mean after that humbling experience, probably the victim should be given the name of an inanimate object or a verb. How about, "Socks", "Hammer", "Rocky" or "Nervous" for instance. In that regard, probably my real name, given that I have so generously been the recipient of such a transformation, should be "Fidgety".

But before I could defend myself or voice any rebuttal or defense, Flo again put the entire matter into its proper perspective. "As usual, Greg, here, made an innocent suggestion. And for some reason, one that I'd rather not go into at this moment, Rita and Jennifer got upset. But I never heard any remarks made from either of them about being offended. How is that possible anyway? Just look at Greg.... (There then was a rather uncomfortable pause as everyone did just that... even a couple of strangers passing through the car at that moment stared at me as if I'd just bitten someone. That made me so nervous I made a vain attempt to smile, which is never easy nor reassuring for a dog to do. We don't have the right facial muscles to successfully accomplish it and end up just showing more teeth... like we're getting hungry.).

Shaking her head, as if looking at me was just about the last thing on Bernie's mind at that moment, she turned back to Rita, Jennifer and Flo, and said, "RIGHT! That's it!! ALL of you march into our cabin this instant. Wally! Close their compartment door! We'll have the porter make up their beds in the morning and tell him to leave it that way for the entire trip. It will only be a sitting room. And for the next two nights the four of you will be sleeping in our room."

And thus ended this rather disturbing incident within the Wagoner's relationships. It puzzled me for months to come, because it marked a change. It signaled that something was afoot. Freedom of speech and action, which was now possible for just about all living creatures and beings of any size, was having a strange and troubling aftereffect.   But I couldn't define exactly what it was.

Probably I initially thought that our endless travels and stunning adventures had numbed my senses enough to blur any chance to think and analyze rationally.   Besides, I usually left that sort of right brain activity up to Flo.   She often told me she thought I was a truly unique variant, possibly the only one of its kind: someone born with only a left-sided brain…

Anyway, we were thoroughly chastened and left with no recourse but to woefully follow Bernie into their bedroom, with Wally bringing up the rear, his wand fully deployed and at the ready to use on any of the four of us. Once we entered their bedroom suite, we were given instructions by Sophie as to where we should lay down. And wouldn't you know, I got the floor space in the shower stall.   Rita was to perch on the sink next to the shower; Jennifer was instructed to sleep under the room's lower bunk bed and Flo was to lie as best she could, squeezing onto the closet floor.   Her size meant that she was more or less half in and half out.

But all of that didn't seem to matter too much because she and I were to spend most of the second leg of our trip back to Seattle in the Lounge Car.   It again had seats that faced outward onto the passing scenery, which suited Flo and I just fine.   It gave us a place and time to reminisce about our lives before we met and about what all had happened afterwards.   It sealed a bond that was unspoken before but was to be everlasting thereafter.

Whatever you have experienced about dogs, cats, birds and any other household "pets", it could easily be said that dogs, of all God's creatures… even the human kind… know more about loyalty than all the rest combined. And as I was to eventually discover, it was something becoming more and more in short supply each and every day throughout this land and its people.

But I digress, because it was only a day or so after this dustup that the second noteworthy event occurred during the second leg of our cross-country, railroad trip. Everyone had settled into a kind of mid-flight routine... as any seasoned traveler might describe it. Meals for Rita, Jennifer, Flo and I were prepared and served in Wally, Bernie, Sophie and Frank's salon... where all of us slept at night. The four, upright bipeds took the time and effort to prepare whatever was being served in the train's Diner for each of us.

Animal and birds' rights advocates had not yet become energized enough to seek equal civil rights for us by this time in the advent of our ability to speak. And my guess would be that a train's Dining Car would be one the last bastions to fall. Dogs slurping turtle soup (to say nothing about how objectionable the thought of that appeals to me) from a fine china, soup terrine, resting on a sparkling, white, linen table cloth, as the sun is setting behind the Black Hills of North Dakota, wouldn't make for a treasured, lifetime memory from some newly-wed couple, who might have been sitting next to me.

But don't get me wrong: I hate not being able to secure, prepare and serve my own food. Sadly, I am not like a wolf, roaming the forests of Siberia, who so easily can do so. Honestly, though, I actually have the hunting instinct of a rock. Still, my dependency on others is a worry, because I ALWAYS have to measure, at least to some degree, my actions and words around others. Unless, of course, I had to resort to dining on the less fortunate, smaller, slower or weaker than me, all of which has no appeal to me whatsoever. And as I looked out the Lounge

Car windows that last, late afternoon of our trip, sitting with Flo, I had the disturbing sensation that maybe what was evolving in the society we were streaking through was a kind of figurative consumption of one another. For the first time I began to have a sensation of pending chaos and irresolvable division in this land we had so tirelessly traveled through once before with Walt and Po.

But before I could enlarge upon that thought, Wally came running up to me, squealing at the top of his seven-year old voice, "Mister Greg, you're needed immediately in our sleeping room! Frank and Sophie need to speak to you right away!! Hurry!!!"

"What about me?" Flo immediately replied, not giving me a moment to consider or question this unusual outburst and request, coming from the most unlikely of messengers.

"No, not you Flo," Wally countered. "For some reason, they only need Greg, here. And it is very urgent!"

Breaking away from my reverie, I looked at Flo and did one of my more dramatic imitations of a shrug... *which, by the way, isn't easy for us dogs to perform*, and said, "Oh, ok, Wally... but I can't imagine what kind of emergency would be helped by me being there."

Rushing back to our sleeper compartment with Wally, as we opened the door, he then added breathlessly, "Upps..., wait a minute, Mister Greg. I may have gotten the message wrong. Come to think of it, maybe it wasn't here I was suppose to rush you."

"Wally!" I exclaimed. "What is going on? Is there an emergency ANYWHERE?"

"Well, I think so," he replied, his reserve providing me no reassurance at all. In fact, I began to flash back to our time together just before climbing aboard the Polar

Wind, that awful night on Seattle's Coast Guard dock when he disappeared the entire ship. "But maybe I was to take you back in the other direction to the Dining Car. I forget."

"So you mean we have to run all the way back the other way?" I snapped.

"Fraid so, Mister Greg," he answered.

And so we did. But I was more than a little peeved at my closest buddy. By now, it was time for him to get any directions and messages straight. He was, after all, the Heir-Apparent Wizard of the Universe. But soon enough, it all became too evident what was going on.

In the time it took for us to dash back and forth through the length of the entire train and pause midway for Wally to realize he had supposedly goofed up, one half of the Lounge Car had been hurriedly transformed. There were ribbons and balloons draped everywhere, bottles and containers of all kinds of food arranged on a make-shift table, and all the Wagoners eagerly facing us as we entered the area again, shouting in one voice: "HAPPY BIRTHDAY!" Unbeknownst to me, April 27th was my seventh birthday. And that day was the 27th. Somehow, Bernie and Wally had found this out. Even I had no idea. It was to be my very first birthday party.

And to begin with, we ate. Somehow, from somewhere, and in a timeframe that bewilders me to this day, the Wagoners had assembled huge mounds of food and various drinks for the celebration. There were salads, main dishes, fruits, veggies for the few that cared for such, treats, ice cream cartons of all flavors, a huge triple-layered rum cake with seven candles on it and bottles of champagne and apple cider. And all around the table, windows and chairs were festooned with balloons, crepe paper and ribbons, with music blaring from an electronic device of some kind that Bernie was given by one of the train's employees.

It was the most exciting time I ever knew... before or since. And I just kept running around in between bites of food and slurps of champagne from a lovely pewter bowl giving everyone sloppy licks and nuzzles. And this went on for at least two hours... enough time, anyway, for me to be told by Sophie that my speech was becoming quite slurred.

Finally, in a moment of sincerest gratitude, I somehow climbed up on one end of the banquet table, where some of the empty food dishes had been removed by Frank and with all the courtliness left in me, swaying as I said it, I pronounced to my dearest friends in the world, "Ev'ry..body, les'n up... I'v got som'ting to say...." But I never finished whatever it was I was going to say, because I fell off the table on top of Jennifer, who bless her heart, because it was my special day, didn't proceed to scratch out both my eyes. Instead, she dragged me over to a nearby armchair, put her one paw around my shoulder and cuddled me.

It was at this point that Wally stood up and addressed everyone. I guess you could say it was the more formal part of the party that was about to begin.

It was just too bad that a major part of me had already left... Being daffy anyway and having too much to drink only added to my sense of having so many separate and distinct personalities all vying inside me in an attempt to present an intact organism of at least minimal intelligence. It was going to take a supreme amount of Walt-Wally wizardry to bring blurry bits of me back to consciousness.

And it all started when Wally announced that he

had a birthday gift for me. This being the only time I EVER had such; a new and more humble reality began to clear my head. For me? A gift? This was a TRUE wonder. Immediately, my tongue hung out the side of my mouth, which then instituted an almost automatic drool. (Not a pretty sight, I realize.) But you must understand I was excited… and a little drunk.

"Greg," Wally began, "after much thought and consultation with my grandfather, Walter, both before and after his death, (which upon the hearing the phrase 'after his death', I think my circulatory system suddenly neutralized all remaining alcohol…) I also consulted with Bernie, and we agreed that it was the proper time to present you with this gift I am now holding. And if you like, I will be glad to help you open the wrapping paper."

Two things sprung into mind at that point: no hands equals need help, and my first gift equals I want no help; it's mine. However, there followed a mental image of my snarling and thrashing the beautifully wrapped box back and forth to try and open it. Whereupon, I looked at Wally and whispered, "Would you please?"

"Sure thing," he whispered back.

And this exchange was followed by our quickly pulling off the ribbon and me giving an eager tug at one end of it, while Wally pulled the tape off the other. Deftly, he pulled the wrapping paper off and let me flip the box's lid off onto the table, now surrounded by everyone either sitting around or on it.

Peering down into it, I saw what had to be one of the most unwanted objects I ever wanted to see, much less have as a gift. It was non-descript, leather-appearing, but having a mixed-color, matching my own black-gray-whitish coat. And sure enough it even had a ring on it; one that a leash of some kind could be attached onto. In horror, I backed away and looked up at Wally with fear and panic. Was this a trick? Had I finally upset everyone enough that they wanted to restrict my access and freedom of movement?

Anticipating this reaction, Wally then spoke. "No one here has seen what you just now did. Here, let me get it out to show them."

And picking it up out of the box, he held it up for everyone to see. He even passed it around the room for everyone to hold and twist around. To me it appeared just as plain and ugly as any other I had ever noticed on other dogs. But when it had been passed around to everyone and Sophie went to hand it to me, Wally intervened quickly.

"No, Greg is not to touch this! It is extremely important that he never has that chance. And it must never be taken off or fall off. You see, Greg, it is a magical collar. It has qualities unheard of and never before seen in any other object on this world. Using it in the proper manner, you will be able to see the future, but you can only do so in the most pivotal moments. It is almost as a last resort for you to do so, depending on the circumstances. It will serve to give you uncommon awareness of what is about to happen, accompanied by insight as to what should be done. It will then allow Bernie, myself and the other Wagoners to assist you."

And with that, in a move so swift and puzzling, he took it from Sophie and with the flick of his hands the collar was suddenly around my neck and once in place I could not feel its presence. It was like I had no awareness of wearing it; like it disappeared.

"You will notice by now," Wally continued, "that you have no feeling of wearing it. Nor will you ever. It will never cause you any discomfort or conscious awareness of its presence.   And to use it you have three options: scratch the right side of it with your right hind leg, the left side with your left hind leg and the top of it by rolling on your back like I've seen you do when you want to scratch your back.

"When you scratch with your right leg, you will be given the power to see what is ahead for you personally. Scratch with your left, and you will see what is going to happen locally or regionally to each of us Wagoners. And, most importantly, scratch the topside of the collar and you will be privileged to know what is to happen on a national scale.   But remember: it is done only for the most dire emergencies."

Dumbstruck, I asked him if I could tell anyone what I saw or heard or felt afterwards, and he replied that I could.   It was to provide an early warning system for everyone.

I was now to become the Official Guard Dog... for everything and everybody.   And boy did that sober me up quickly.   I even briefly wondered if I should have a uniform of some kind to wear as well.   Something to maybe coordinate with Jennifer's lovely outfits...

And as if to confirm the appropriateness of the gift, after I had thanked nearly everyone, starting with giving Wally a slurpy lick and a heart-felt "thank you"; by the time I made it back to where Jennifer and I had been huddled, I ran up to her, and she politely shook her head that my gesture wasn't necessary for her, but quickly added, "I know you're very grateful and happy, and you have every right to be, old friend.   And most of all, your new collar suits you.   It makes a lovely accessory."

THREE: R AND R TURNS INTO TRAGEDY

In my own mind, it hadn't been long enough since us Wagoners had finished our cross-country, adventurous trip of discovery and reformation, followed almost immediately with our around-the-world voyage and then to try and sort out all that had happened over these past months to have completely recovered physically and mentally.

In fact, it had only been three months since we got back from our train trip from New York City. I remember the day well; it was July 28th, when the surprise of all surprises occurred. What was it? Captain Shriver and his family stopped by Willa's to see us. And he brought Happy. Now... there was one transformed ship's mascot. It appeared that even when he is not on board some ship-of-sea, he kept trying to muster whoever or whatever was in his immediate vicinity for formation and roll call.

And seeing the purposefulness and crisp uniform of Polar Wind's ship captain and his deliriously dutiful dog, I became overly jealous and began to sulk. Frankly, I'd be one of the first to admit that our missions of total world transformations had left me, in particular, with the ever-growing feeling of being cast off or a has-been. Honestly, in the midst of all those adventures, I had become a kind of action-junkie. But what I didn't know, being the type who keeps these kind of feelings to himself, was that Rita, Jennifer, Flo, Wally, Bernice and Sophie were also beginning to feel like attic antiques, has-been heroes or retired reformers.

Only Frank had used the time since we returned to Willa's to try and make himself useful. He had decided to run for office as a State Representative. He believed fervently in "Greg's Plan", the one I outlined on our wagon trip. Frank was running for office as a nonpartisan and was meeting overwhelming opposition for this in Washington, D.C. and in Olympia, our State Capitol. But, if nothing else, Frank was doggedly determined (*if I may take the liberty to use such a word in this context*). Much of what had happened since those earliest days in Atlantic City would not have happened without his steadfast and persistent nature to get a job done. According to him, a grass roots upheaval was beginning to take shape regionally and nationally, and it was becoming more and more defined each day.

Anyway, sensing my uneasiness with Happy's endless parading and purposefulness, Flo came over and asked if I was ok; and I replied, obviously still smarting, that I felt Happy's behavior gave us dogs a bad image.

And believe me, now that everyone and everything that surrounds you talks, has opinions, makes demands and whines... image IS all-important. Practically everything you see or hear is now either mumbling, advising, pontificating, bellowing or strutting. I even briefly thought about suggesting that we should ask Wally if he could perform a case-by-case, species reversal of Walt's and his transformations. I briefly thought that using his wand, staff or some weird incantation, even here with us so isolated at Willa's, he could pinpoint some needed alterations on this ship-of-sea dog. Seeing this squirmy dog being both so busy and so unflappably regimented gave me the deepest sense of being lost.

But don't get me wrong. Despite these insecure feelings and doubts, I couldn't help but still be aware that much had been happening in the last three months throughout our nation. And Captain Shriver and his wife, Stella, confirmed it.

And while it's true that Frank had been trying to tell me that there were still many unsettling issues in the public arena, I wrongly assumed that because that news was coming from Frank, who had never shown a reformer's zeal for changing the status quo, it had not made much of a dent in my self-pity or inspired me to crusade for further change. Besides, I had been too busy becoming depressed, especially now that I was witnessing the twit-like activity of Happy. Even ever-steady Flo had rolled her eyes at me once or twice since the Shriver's had arrived. Only Willa and Sophia seemed thrilled at their unexpected arrival or so we thought it had been.

Come to find out, Willa... at Sophie's suggestion... had prearranged the entire affair. *I should have known.*

All the while I had been cruising in the nearby woods with Flo, Jennifer and Rita, a magnificent dinner had been prepared and laid out for our guests anticipated arrival. As one might expect knowing her as I do now, Sophie had set seating cards out for everyone around Willa's mammoth table.

My guess was that she did so to prevent any

squabbles and snarling. As always, she anticipated the age-old issue of animal and bird kingdom dominance issues.

However, she over-looked one potential conflict, one simmering due to my insecure feelings now nearing volcanic proportions: she had arranged for Happy to sit directly across from me. And it's timely to also note here, for anyone reading this report at some point, that Wally's silly collar had become completely dismissed from my mind. I didn't feel it, and I never have the need to look at myself in mirrors, so I never saw it. It simply didn't exist any longer, but ever-snappy, Happy did; and he kept staring at it throughout the dinner. We never exchanged any words. He just kept staring. Finally, just as desert was about to be served, I snapped.

"What are you staring at, YOU POMPOUS WART?!!" I suddenly yelled.

And what immediately followed was like someone poureing warm molasses over the entire gathering, right up to their necks. Everyone froze in place, saying nothing… momentarily at least. It was Willa who broke that smoldering silence first.

"GREG!!! LEAVE THE TABLE AT ONCE!!! YOU ARE A BAD DOG!!"

Now then. First off, I'd never heard Willa shout like that. So that took me completely by surprise. BUT, NO ONE, and I mean NO ONE had ever called me a "BAD DOG", at least not since Howard did long ago in Atlantic City.

I think then it was associated with my completely shredding his brand new sofa one day when he and his family left me locked in the house, while they went down to the Pier for the day. I had been known to run off for days at a time, and Howard was understandably tired of it. But being me, I didn't feel contrite about my absences and decided to show him a thing or two. It wasn't right, and it still bothers me. I probably should have had Sophie send him money to pay for a new one, but I don't ever earn any. And even if I did, how could I hold onto whatever I earned. Paws with claws don't make for easy handling of anything. So that leaves me with using my mouth way too much... as I did that night at the Shriver's welcoming dinner. Thoroughly chastised, I slunk off my stool and crept into Willa's parlor room. She was right; I was a bad dog.

Oddly enough, it was Captain Shriver who first came to look in on me and sat down next to where I was lying. And thankfully, he had the good sense not to let Happy tag along. Sitting down in one of Willa's Hoosier armchairs, he reassured me in a way that I witnessed him do so many times on our around-the-world trip.

"These are tough times aren't they, old fella. And I know that Happy's unquenchable desire to be the most eager and alert individual present in any gathering is at the very least annoying. It's like he is always 'on duty', and no one can do whatever needs to be done better. It can be really irritating... even to me. When people get like that, I sometimes want to jump overboard. And I had the feeling you were taking a leap just now at the dinner table. Am I right?"

"Yes, sir. But instead of going overboard, I always seem to leap head-long into trouble with my runaway mouth. I'm trying to do better about my impatience and outspokenness, but people and critters like Happy just seem to pull an emotional hair-trigger of mine. Please apologize to him for me. And I know I'm going to have to apologize to Willa and Sophie. Boy! Was Willa mad!"

"She sure was. But I'm sure she'll be ok as soon as this dinner is over. I'll speak with her. Don't worry."

And with that, I did a very unusual and out-of-character gesture: I got up and slowly walked around and rested my chin on his leg.

And sure enough he did speak with Willa and Sophie, and there was no further mention of my outburst. In fact Willa came to me first and asked if I thought it would be a good idea to ask everyone if they would like to go on a picnic. My immediate response was that it was a great idea, and that I knew just the spot to have it. She immediately agreed and said that once the table was cleared, she would enlist everyone to help prepare for our heading out tomorrow about 10 a.m. She would have Jimmy get his bus ready and tell everyone about our plan.

It was a relief for me to be in her good graces again. And I vowed NEVER to speak again at one of these dinner parties. I was going to be a "good" dog, even if I had to wear a muzzle at those dinnertime functions.

That next morning was filled with all the beauty and promise that the highest, snow-capped Olympic Mountains and the unparalleled size and density of the mammoth Hoh Rainforest trees and dense undergrowth could provide. The sky was so blue and clear it heightened the color of everything around us. The reds were redder; the greens were of infinite shades, some almost black and others so pale they faded from sight; the pastures were a harvest-yellowish brown, indicating that summer's respite from the relentless rains to come was almost at hand. And everywhere there were the wildflowers, each variety seemingly competing to be the brightest and most luscious for any passing bee. Any direction you looked was a vista waiting to be painted. It was to be a perfect day… or so I thought.

And by 10 a.m., just as Willa had commanded, all of us were loaded aboard Jimmy's tour bus, along with our baskets of picnic supplies, blankets and some pillows. There were eighteen of us, all tucked snugly into the bus. And as usual, the representatives of the animal and bird kingdoms immediately scampered in and hopped up onto the wide wooden shelves that Jimmy had so conveniently installed for the tourists' snacks, cameras and purses. Besides the eight original Wagoners, there were Willa, Capt. Shriver, Stella, Happy, Jimmy, Diane, Margaret, Helen, Jules, Tom and me.

It was a merry crew, to say the least. Singing began almost immediately upon everyone getting settled. The brightness that remarkably clear day and the uncommon warmness that enveloped you courtesy of the delicious sunshine, which was often rarely seen or enshrouded in thick coastal fog or clouds, made for a festive and glorious occasion.

Our trip was to be about thirty miles to the Olympic National Park's Rialto Beach, adjacent to the La Push Indian Reservation on the Pacific Coast. (see Appendix: **Rialto Beach**) It's a stunning beach area, accessible most safely by trail, one which winds through the forest and then down a two hundred foot cliff face. To access this beach area solely by walking along the shoreline is dangerous, at best, given the unpredictable rough seas and rip tides in the area. Willa had often told us of the area, but none of us had ever been there before. All of us were thrilled to be going. Excitement and anticipation was almost off any scale of how one might measure such.

Once we arrived at the designated parking area for this particular beach access, each of us was assigned something to bring to the picnic area. The only exception was Rita. She had to ride on top of Flo, who still had her set of saddle bags, especially made by Sophie for him and me... if you remember. She even had an extra one that fit on Happy. Each set of bags had pockets for refreshments, cutlery and ground cloths. Baskets of food, blankets and umbrellas were carried by the more upright members of our excited expedition. We were all feeling so joyous and excited that the singing had kept up until we first came to what was to be the most remarkable sanctuary I have ever entered.

Picture, if you will, walking completely unprepared from bright sunshine and a cloudlessly clear blue sky into an area shrouded in twilight. There was no gradual transition. Your first step into the mile-long expanse of forest that you must wind your way through to get to the steep bluff leading down to the sea plunged you into a sanctuary that appeared ageless. Its threshold was like nothing any of us had ever seen before.

Scattered everywhere before us were countless remnants of old growth stumpage, logged off probably one hundred years ago. But the most stunning sight was not seeing the ravages of this harvest; but instead, it was seeing the resulting rebirth. There were countless rotting and crumbling, immense stumps scattered everywhere from this ancient forest. And most remarkable of all, the stumpage had daughter trees growing up out of them or around them. Often it looked like the renewed growth of these younger trees was trying to cover over or hide their parent's stumpage. It was a classic example of nature trying to recover from some senseless act of carnage. And the absolute silence only added to the reverential tone of this place. You see, in these Northwest, most ancient of forests, there are normally very few birds and animals at any time. It's as if even they know this is a very special place. You come here only on the most urgent or blessed occasions.

These ancient forests should never have been treated as an economic windfall, as a product to harvest. They, above all things living deserved to be left alone. Harvest their cousins' further inland, but not these most majestic of life forms. And most remarkable of all to me, none of them spoke... unlike what other trees were now doing the world over after Walt and Wally's stupefying transformations.

It was like the other trees knew that this was a special place, where silence was to be their true voice. There was a majesty in this place that was unlike any I had experienced anywhere else. And the canopy was so dense that daylight hardly entered. We almost needed flashlights to find our way. Certainly, if the sun had not been as bright as it was, we would have probably needed them.

And as luck would have it, we did find a clearing off to one side of the main trail, which lead to the edge of the bluff's overlook. It was Flo who led the way to that prize spot. Her keen instinct of knowing the best and safest route to take... in any situation... guided us to the area. Later we found this spot was not indicated on any hiking map.

It was a grassy area, about one acre in diameter. Bordering it were the new growth trees, emerging out of and around the decaying stumpage. If the dense forest was the sanctuary, this clearing was certainly to be our chapel. And looking out, unimpeded, onto the mighty Pacific Ocean was a sight like none other I had ever known.

It was wondrous. Pillars of ancient sea stacks studded the water in front of us. Some of them were the size of small islands maybe fifty to one hundred feet high. Tide pools were evident around some of the ones closer to the shoreline when the tide was out. The sandy beach itself was at least fifty yards deep, once you left the bottom of the steep bluff's winding pathway. And as was the custom in these parts, all beaches are left stacked with clumps of driftwood logs, some piled as high as ten feet; and this one was no exception.

The only sound, other than that of the spiritual silence of the forest behind us, was that of the gentle sloshing of the surf. The sea was matching the tone of the beautiful day above and around us. There was absolute peacefulness and quiet... coupled with the cooing of the incoming waves.

After each of us had taken the time to survey the open area, pausing varying lengths of time to gaze out on the vista before us and just drink in the beauty of this day, we reassembled and began to spread out the ground cloths, baskets and collapsible armchairs for our once-in-a-lifetime, ocean-front picnic. The mood and anticipation could not have been loftier and more thankful. It was for me the perfect moment.

And then it began. And for the life of me, I cannot recall the first indication that something of earth-moving significance was about to occur. Maybe it was the depth of the silence, as if all nature knew a secret that was too awful to even whisper to anyone. Even the ocean itself seemed to become muted, too afraid and horrified about what was about to happen to make any sound. But honestly, the only real memory I have was of an almost imperceptible rolling under my feet and then everyone jerking their heads around in shock to see and hear Flo, Happy and I begin to bark and howl a most mournful wail for some unexplainable reason.

Because immediately thereafter, there began a mounting series of explosive shakes and the most violent rocking anyone could imagine. No one could stand. All of us were thrown to the ground. Only Rita was privileged enough to launch herself skyward to avoid being injured. At one point in the five to six minute unrelenting horror of listening to what could only be described as hearing the earth tear itself open, I managed to look over and see the adults and children rolling side to side and bouncing to and fro. I could only imagine that some or all of them were having bones break. Even Flo was being bounced up and down like she was a rubber ball.

And most horrifying of all, everyone's mouths were wide open, screaming in panic with all the volume their lungs would allow. It was a time of sheer and absolute terror. I was sure that the bluff we were on was going to collapse into the sea. And sure enough much of the land at its edge did collapse. It was only by some unforeseen miracle that we had moved well back into that clearing to prepare for our picnic. And the other blessing was that the trees surrounding that area had not achieved much height. As I thought about it later, I figured the moisture they would normally get from the endless rainfall probably seeped down the escarpment before it could get to their roots.

Beyond being badly shaken and more terrified than anyone could imagine, when the noise and shaking stopped, we found that no one was seriously injured. But seeing the faces of Wally and Bernie, I knew that something even more horrifying was about to occur.

Standing up, each of us... for some unknown reason... turned our attention to the ocean. For fear of further collapse of the cliff face, we stayed back a safe distance. But it still allowed us a clear vista for tens of miles of shoreline in either direction. And at first it seemed calm and undisturbed by all this violence.

But it was Wally who spoke first. "Look, Mr. Greg, the water seems to be leaving the beach. Why is that?"

Of course I had no idea, but then Willa spoke up and with fear and mounting panic in her voice and announced, "Look, everyone, see the white line across the horizon. What is it?"

It was Bernie who replied to both these questions. Her herald status and its accompanying ability gave her the insight and presence of mind to analyze what was occurring better than any of the rest of us. "It's a tsunami!"

It was Frank who then pronounced the benediction for the day and for the times that were ahead for all of us. "May God have mercy on us. This earthquake was the disaster predicted that would someday occur, and now it has. What now is about to occur will change everything for everybody for the rest of our lives... for those of us who even survive what is about to happen."

Aghast already, and then even becoming more terrified, we watched the approaching white line; some of us muttering prayers, others moaning, and each of us clinging to someone nearby. There was no way any us to know or determine how big or how high the incoming waves would be. We could only hope they would be small and of no consequence. We were wrong.

With each new one, the series of waves that occurred over the next fifteen minutes grew in size. At first the smaller islands in front of us disappeared in their onrush. But by the last wave the biggest stack in front of us almost disappeared in blue water, and once that wave hit the bluff below us, there was even splashing water that surged up and over us. Captain Shriver estimated after it passed that the wave itself had to be somewhere between one hundred and one hundred and fifty feet high! Only being on that high bluff saved us! And there was no way at that moment to estimate the damage and loss of life that was then occurring for tens to hundreds of miles around us.

The sky was still azure blue; the trees still standing were still lush and green, but we knew the earth around us was going to be mired in destruction and death like none of us would have ever imagined.

It was at that point, once we had stopped screaming and crying that Wally came over to me and whispered, "Mr. Greg, I need you to scratch your neck with your right hind leg. We need to know what is going to be happening around us, as frightful and terrible as I fear it will be."

THE FIRST VISION

FOUR: OVERFLIGHT

It was immediately clear to each of us, some of whom were either huddled together or others tossed haphazardly into a contorted sprawl on the ground, that something beyond terrible had just occurred. No one had spoken up until then, but undoubtedly each of us were screaming and yelling throughout this entire ravaging onslaught of nature. Not even during the silence leading up to the tsunami waves striking the coast did anyone speak; at that point everyone just moaned and cried. And once the waves began to strike the coastline, our wailing began anew.

It was like witnessing the destruction of a world. Nothing in all likelihood throughout the history of this continent, as it is presently formed geologically, had anything of this magnitude been witnessed. This unparalleled onslaught of nature, her sheer detachment and neutrality during its advent and the staggering aftermath, left you paralyzed and vacant. It was like the void of deep space, with all its impartial disregard for life, had suddenly exploded into our lives. Cosmic and natural disasters have no compassion and seek no absolution. They are the unrehearsed, physical order of Universal existence. They are the real order of things. And it left us numbed to our individual cores.

It was Captain Shriver who finally spoke, as if his years of command had dictated that he assume some management role in responding to what had just occurred. "Is anyone hurt?" he asked. "Please, each of you call out that they are ok or not."

Dazed beyond only being able to respond with one or two word replies, each of us acknowledged our conscious presence.

As to the question as to whether we were ok, it was only too clear that none of us would probably ever be that again. We'd seen a devastating and ominous rehearsal for the final act of this world's, ballooning population. Extermination events are cyclic and inevitable. They're the rule. At that very moment when the earth shook so violently and then these waves struck, we each knew that our presence on this world was purposeful and by the grace of something Infinite, but it was also temporary and the exception.

Having an abiding faith and religious conviction cements one's soul within a hope of something beyond the destruction that we were witnessing and will witness in the days, months and years ahead. But neither will prevent what we saw from becoming reoccurring nightmares nor will they lessen the anguish we felt in those moments. Just looking around me, I could see that each of us was being tested to his or her limit. Your first impulse was to start screaming with all that resided in you... and never stop. You hoped your voice would carry across the indifferent void of all time and space and halt this unstoppable madness of natural events. But you knew it would only be swallowed up by indifference. To be forlorn in those moments was to know the reality of universal time and space. Only the fifth dimension of faith offered us any comfort.

"Very well, then" Captain Shriver continued, as if guiding a Coast Guard vessel through angry seas, "we must try and find a way out of here. Rita! If you can and are able, please fly aloft and see if you notice any pathway open enough for us to walk back to Jimmy's bus. Flo! Please check the stability of the cliff edge, now just immediately in front of us. I fear there is to be a landslide soon, given the amount of earth removed by those waves. See how far you think we should back up to be safe. Wally and Bernie! Please consider what we have to do to escape this area if Rita finds there is no way out, using the way we came in or any other way by walking or riding. Sophie and Frank, please check on the others to make sure there are no injuries that need tending. And finally Greg! You and Happy need to scout the immediate area to see if there are any survivors. We mustn't leave anyone behind that might have survived this cataclysm. I'll wait here until each of you report back to me as to what you've discovered."

In summary, there was no escape from our clearing, given the composition of our party. And Happy and I found that there were no survivors in our immediate vicinity. If we had been caught in the woods, no doubt many of us would have perished as well. And certainly everyone walking down the bluff face and enjoying themselves in the tide pools or on the beach was swept away. The destruction around us was appalling.

It was at that point that Wally stopped me from

47

reporting our findings to Captain Shriver and asked Happy to do so. Instead, he asked me to sit and scratch my collar for the first time with my right hind leg. He needed to know if my safety, along with everyone else's, was in immediate peril. Only after knowing we were relatively safe would he then embark on his next option... to leave this forlorn area.

Reluctantly, I did as he requested. But given all that had already happened, I was filled with dread. How could any of us be safe? I was absolutely sure no one else in this region was. But once I scratched as instructed, the vision that slowly came into view was that of us being in flight. There was no sense of danger or injury to me... at least for the immediate future. And then I was fully awake. It all happened so quickly and painlessly, I hardly grasped the urgency of it performing the maneuver.

Shaking my head, as if to clear my thoughts, I then reported what I saw to Wally. He just nodded his head in relief, and then called everyone over to join us.

After our group had reassembled and the various reports were given, Bernie finally spoke on what she and Wally determined was the only course left for us to escape this area. Wally would have to unsheathe his ever-trusty wand and transform each of us... except Rita... into birds, and then we'd have to fly out of this clearing. It seemed logical, but for those of us who had not experienced this alteration, it created a mild panic. Even Willa was skeptical and objected.

That amazed me, given her extended lifetime with Walt and no doubt seeing all the bewildering transformations he must have concocted over their time together. Still, even Flo and I looked at each other with some anxiety. To go from lifelong, ground sniffers to mammalian flyers in split seconds is not the customary evolutionary progression.

But we knew if Bernie said it was necessary, it had to be done. And almost immediately as she mentioned it, before any objections became too resistant or hostile, Wally had altered each of us in our picnic party into Canadian Geese.

Of course, there followed the expected gasps and moans from the uninitiated but were not heard from us Wagoners. We were no longer newbie's to this wacky world of wizardry and had already experienced these same abrupt transformations as we crossed the country and then the world.

But don't let me minimize the absolute seriousness and tragedy of the time at hand and what was to lie ahead. I'm not trying to be callous. If anything, my comments at this point are part of what Flo and I call "Dog Humor" or what some of you might call "Gallows Humor". It's strictly a less-than-optimal coping mechanism in times of terrible stress.

And immediately my reverie was interrupted by Wally, the Transformer-in-Chief, who had now taken charge of this upcoming migration by his announcing, "Ok, follow me. I believe I know what Greg needs to observe first-hand before he has to initiate his second, most-important vision. Stay in formation behind and to the side of me, if you will. We must all stay together. You must never lose sight of me; otherwise this transformative process weakens, given the number of us there are. I don't want anyone falling out of the sky."

Now that got my attention. Immediately, I decided that I was going to fly wingtip-to-wingtip next to him. And so did everyone else...

Our jumbled attempt at flying in any kind of formation was mob-like; somewhat like a ruffled collection of feathers, beaks and web feet thrashing aimlessly in mid-air. And once we were fully aloft, Wally had to shout, "Will you PLEASE separate and get into some kind of recognizable formation. You're embarrassing me!"

Well, try this sometime yourself... scared out of our wits already, and then trying to grasp the concept of formation flying, along with having just experienced what later was to be called the most destructive earthquake in recorded or prehistory. We were not exactly ready for a full-dress parade with accompanying martial music. Each of us was really scared... even panic-stricken.

Wally was just going to have to guide and coax us along. And after circling a few times at low altitude over the previously heavily forested area we had been hiking through, we were ready to head south along what used to be the original coastline. But NOTHING was the same, nor would it ever be in anyone's lifetime that had just experienced that previous fifteen minutes of horror.

As soon as we achieved any altitude, the resulting devastation became fully visible. Wherever the cliffs or bluffs hadn't been over 150 feet high the onrushing water, which must have been moving at a staggering speed, roared inland for miles in some places. And the land it scoured was now barren. Whitish gray sand and subsoil was all that remained. Denuded of all vegetation, essentially all the magnificent cedars, hemlock and fir trees were gone! Looking westward, as we flew further south, you could see that the ocean was now a floating graveyard, covered for as far out as we could scan with the detritus of this once pristine region.

Luckily, there were very few settlements or

communities along the shoreline in this immediate vicinity. But sadly, adding to their historically tragic history of being abused and slaughtered between themselves and later by so-called "colonizers", the Native Indian villages that were clumped along the Olympic Peninsula's, ocean coastline, had all disappeared as well. No one could have possibly survived the towering waves.

And as we flew further south, Wally called out to me to come up close beside him. He wanted me there, along with Bernie who was already on his other side, to document what we saw. Our formation by this time resembled a perfect "V", with Frank and Captain Shriver at each trailing end of the split. They maneuvered themselves there to insure the safety of any stragglers. If the circumstances had been much different, it would have been a pleasant sight to see. As it was, our tidy flight formation sharply contrasted the destruction evolving below us, as the inland flood waters slowly receded back into the ocean.

However, it wasn't until we were approaching the larger communities and cities at the southern end of the Peninsula that the true magnitude of this horrific event became only too clear. Cities on the flat sandbars, like Ocean Shores, Westport, South Bend and Long Beach had been scraped away. There was no indication they ever even existed. Cities further inland like Hoquiam, Aberdeen and Astoria were also gone, but instead of having vanished, all that remained were hundred-feet-high piles of rubble. The endless miles of their proud communities were strewn up against their surrounding hillsides as far as we could see.

Swooping lower, being ever led by Wally, we did see the beginnings of survivors gradually stumbling out from and around the tangled mass of their communities; but there were not many. There just wasn't time to escape to high enough ground to avoid the gigantic waves that followed the earthquake's massive shaking. We later learned that it was a 9.7 quake! From all we could see, too few would survive what happened at its epicenter to ever tell others. (see Appendix: **Cascadian Fault**)

From there we continued to fly along the denuded coastline down as far as Crescent City, California, beyond which, for all we could tell in those earliest moments, the heaviest destruction seemed to play itself out... or at least so we thought. With this latest earthquake and tsunami, most of that city was wiped out as well.

And then Wally turned, headed inland and back in a northerly direction over the sparsely populated and traveled coastal mountain range. It wasn't until we reached the Portland metropolitan area that we began to see the dramatic effects of the earthquake again. Here, fires were still burning uncontrollably and even the tallest structures had collapsed, including the bridges which spanned the Columbia River. To me, it all looked like an unimaginable tangled mess.

Then, only adding to the trauma and devastation of what we had seen thus far, Wally led us up the Interstate 5 corridor over the Olympia, Tacoma, Seattle, Everett, Bellingham and Vancouver metropolitan areas. None of us could believe what we were seeing. Apparently, the tsunami waves were about fifty feet high when they entered the Strait of Juan de Fuca; high enough certainly to erase most of Port Angeles, Victoria and Bellingham. But, to our continued amazement, the ferocity of it all became even more destructive. Between the earthquake and the tidal waves, which were still 25 feet high when they struck Seattle and Bremerton, the damage to these two cities was in the 60-75% range. Their docks were totally destroyed, as was much of Seattle's downtown. The same was true for Bremerton. The loss of life was staggering. And the full extent of the earthquake extended all the way up to and through Vancouver.

From all indications, this region now lay in ruins. The Northwest was in shambles. Frank's interest in running for office appeared fruitless. How could he get around? Who was there to vote for him? On what platform would he run? How could he get staffers to help him? Who would they be anyway? And what kind of governing body was left?

Furthermore, I began to worry about how the federal government's agencies could respond appropriately to this massive catastrophe. Their responses to much lesser disasters had been fraught with ineptitude and cloaked in bureaucratic indifference. I knew right away this event was to change EVERYTHING. It was like a war had been declared and the first strike occurred without any warning, and the destruction was total. This was the 'tipping point'. Something so grave and fundamental was about to happen to this beloved country of ours. The years of its fragile and tenuously unified existence were now to be seriously threatened.

FIVE: THE DISRUPTION

There then followed a series of events that signaled the future for everyone was forever going to be changed… for us Wagoners and foe all citizens of These United States.

Our flight concluded with Wally leading us back across the Strait, over what used to be Port Angeles, past the western portion of the Olympic Mountains and then straight down to Willa's farm. Honestly, I was completely exhausted both emotionally and physically from all that had happened and from what we had seen since our aborted picnic and over the course of that lengthy, Wally-generated flight. Being in that state of mind and body, I decided to keep my eyes on Wally, rather than looking down anymore. I had seen too much destruction, as I was sure everyone else had as well. Everyone's spirits had to be frayed.

But just at that point, I heard Willa cry out just as we banked in preparation to head down to her farmhouse. "Oh, no!" she cried. "It's gone! There's nothing left of our farm! The earthquake leveled it all!!"

Just as soon as we landed, Wally instantly had each of us restored to our earthbound selves. And each of us gasped at what we saw.

Willa was wailing inconsolably as she stumbled toward her ruined farm house. It wasn't enough that it was demolished, but it seemed that the earthquake had had a grudge to settle. It appeared to me that what we were seeing was like I what would happen if I had have a piece of rag in my mouth and shook it violently side to side. Pieces of her home were strewn across the surrounding pasture. I sincerely doubt any of us would have survived being in it, given the destruction we saw at that moment. Trees were down everywhere; many lying yards from their original, implanted location. It was as if they were not just knocked down but were then heaved into the air, landing far from their place of origin.

There was a ferocity to all this that was numbing. We later learned that the Cascadia fault line was ripped and rose over forty feet along the ocean floor from Vancouver Island all the way along the Washington and Oregon shorelines. It even caused avalanches, along with steam venting from out of the dormant volcanoes, from Mt. Baker to Mt. Lassen, a distance of over 500 miles. (see Appendix: **Cascade Eruptions During the Past 4,000 Years.**)

From the time the earthquake started, around 1 p.m., until our landing at Willa's destroyed farm that evening around 8: 30 p.m., there was still enough visibility that July night from the Sun not yet fully setting and from the dust having settled that was heaved up during the course of the earth's thrashing to see clearly what damage had been done. Each of us just stood shaking our heads at the total destruction around us. Flying over it all for the last seven hours was heart-wrenching enough, but as with anything, once you are face-to-face with the ruins around you, it becomes very personal.

Willa was inconsolable. Sophie, her daughters and Stella attempted to comfort her, but it was fruitless. The saga of her and Walt's tenure here on this world was rapidly coming to an end. The crumbled mass in front of her signaled her time here was also finished. And eventually her crying stopped, and she just crumbled to the ground, despite Sophie and Diane each trying to hold onto her. Within a matter of minutes, it was clear she had not just swooned from overwhelming grief, but that she was about to bid all of us farewell. We were now about to be on our own. The era of Walt and Willa had come to an end. The mantle was to fall entirely on Bernie and Wally's shoulders from here on.

Lying Willa beside the clump of younger fir trees which she and Walt had planted some fifty years ago, and ones that remarkably had survived the ground shaking, in a whispered voice, Willa asked that her two grandchildren be brought to her.

"Bring them to me, please," she uttered. And because Flo and I were already crouched unobtrusively behind her, we were privileged to hear her last words, once they knelt over her.

"Children," she began. "Your grandfather and I are both so proud of you. We want you to know that. You have done all that we could have hoped you might to bring some tranquility to this weary world. I fear, however, the unimaginable tragedy that struck us this morning will unravel some of your efforts. Still, you must remain steadfast. You have given this world the means, message and hope to heal itself, but hovering over it and amidst it is the unpredictable and ever-present variable of human behavior. Stay alert. Use Greg's visions to help foretell what may be happening around you.

"And now you must move on. There is nothing here to keep you. My guess is that you will find refuge in the Lodge by Lake Quinault, about thirty miles south of here. Go there immediately. Don't tarry here any longer than is necessary.

"Pease place me beside my beloved Walter and go. You are now all that remains of our precious gifts to this world. The loss of your mother was devastating to us both. But you two have filled that loss so ably... despite your youth.

"Now give me a kiss and a hug. My time is over. May God bless and keep you always, my dear ones."

And upon Bernie and Wally leaning over and each kissing her, with tears streaming down their little cheeks, Willa let out a gentle sigh and her body went limp.

Inching around on our bellies, so as not to disturb the children, Flo and I then placed our heads on her outstretched lower legs. And the four of us stayed huddled there for some time, assuring Willa's spirit a gentle farewell and passage.

Some time later, Bernie finally rose and walked over to Frank and Jimmy and asked them to go over to the now-destroyed barn and see if they could find shovels to prepare the gravesite for Willa.

Upon hearing their request, Capt. Shriver asked if he could also help. It was now clear to him that given the immensity of what had happened this day, his duty now was both to his family and to these most uncommon of friends. Their welfare and safety probably was more important than him trying to wander around the devastated docks of what used to be a Coast Guard Station. He saw only too clearly on their earlier over-flight of the Northwest that all coastal facilities had been obliterated. Help and any rebuilding would have to start from the ground up; local seaside assistance was fruitless and impossible. Already, the new world order was powerfully dictating new changes in priorities and very limited means or avenues to meet them.

Meanwhile Stella and Sophie began collecting scattered bits of material to make a shroud and directed others to find material to fashion a casket of some kind. This was to be a formal burial, even in the midst of what had happened that day. Wally and Bernie had been able to locate his collapsible staff, which had been used so successfully on our worldwide journey, amongst the rubble that was once Willa's home. Using it, Wally had been able to facilitate some of the preparations and materials needed, such as engraved headstones for both Walt and Willa, chairs, candles and needed food and water. None of us had eaten or drank anything all day. By nightfall, the gravesite and a most solemn ceremony were completed.

But because all the roads on the Olympic Peninsula had buckled or been blocked and were completely impassable the entire length and width of the Peninsula, Wally informed everyone following Willa's internment that it would be necessary for everyone to become geese again to travel over to the Lodge Willa had suggested should now be their new home. (see Appendix: **Lake Quinault Lodge**). And this time there were no looks or expressions of surprise. Fatigue, shock and grief were taking their toll on each of us. We just hoped there was enough of the Lodge still intact to provide us some shelter for the night.

After the subsequent short flight over to it, Wally led us the short distance to the lawn area and up to its back entrance steps, which are framed by the graceful Lodge. And to our absolute amazement, it appeared structurally sound. As we approached it, once we were transformed back to our usual appearance, we could see there were many broken windows and the entry doors on the back porch were hanging ajar and mangled. And there were stones scattered over the porch and into the lawn area from the chimney that had obviously been toppled during the quake. Otherwise, it appeared safe enough to enter.

Once inside the back entranceway, using flashlights Wally had provided for us during Willa's funeral and were now again made available to us, we could see that everything that once was hanging on the walls or stood upright on the floor were now strewn about. But before too long, we cleared away the fallen or broken items and brushed off the over-stuffed, leather upholstered armchairs and sofas. Then like soldiers who had been fighting endlessly, without a word, each of us found a chair, sofa, carpet or perch and wordlessly collapsed into dreamless sleep for the next fourteen hours.

The next day, on July 30th, after our awakening, brought a series of timely and life-saving miracles, events such as we were to see few of for months to come. Sometime before everyone awakened, Wally had taken both his staff and wand and gone to work on silently repairing the Lodge. Unlike his not doing anything for Willa's destroyed farmhouse, which he later told me was because it was his grandparents, and he had the strongest sense it was time to leave it be. It was like Walt was telling him go forward. You have no time to look back. Willa and I are done here.

And by the time we each had opened our eyes and stretched the first thing we saw was the Lodge in its pristine condition. He had even secured... somehow... a gas generator for electricity. This place was now a haven of safety for anyone in the area to come to and find shelter. And come they did. By noon that day there were at least fifty people who sought shelter with us: registered guests, Lodge employees, neighbors and refugees from nearby villages who had been hiding in the woods or what was left of them.

Wally just beamed when I looked over at him. He knew he'd really done something good this time. *There were to be no more disappearing ships by his hand.* Next, he motioned for me to follow him outside the front door of the Lodge, and there he proudly pointed to a double-cab pickup truck that he restored or found unscathed and had teleported there. But he wasn't done. With a wide grin, he then motioned me out onto the roadway that coursed its way to the only highway that traverses north and south along the entire peninsula.

What I saw was nothing short of a true miracle. He had been able to direct his staff or wand, along with using various Walt/Willa-inspired incantations, and had opened a single lane in the roadway. Trees and boulders of all sizes had been shifted enough to allow a zigzagged, clear passage off into the distance.

"What do you think, Mister Greg?" he asked. "I made an opening for us to drive through all the way around the Peninsula to Bremerton, where I thought Frank might have better luck finding enough people to start helping organize relief and rescue work."

"Wally!" I shouted with glee, "You're a miracle worker for sure. But did you leave any room for other vehicles to pass someone?"

"Sure did," he answered. "I made sure there was a little clearing every so often for just that purpose. Somebody may have to back up a little, but there will be room to pass."

"You are an amazing Wizard," I could only say, which I know really pleased him. And then I ambled over and gave him one of my more meaningful and affectionate leg-rubs.

I would have even given him a first class, dog kiss; but he's getting a little old for that. Besides, licking wizards may have untold consequences. I know it sure did when I tried to do it to Jennifer...

When we got back inside the Lodge, it was clear that despite the grief and bewilderment everyone felt, the need and desire to start bringing some order and relief to others had begun. And the Wagoners, along with Capt. Shriver and Stella, were front and center in that effort. Even Happy volunteered to go out and help find survivors in the surrounding rubble.

That immediately began to change my opinion of him.

After something to eat, Bernie suggested that it might be best if some supplies were put in the back of Wally's pickup truck and that she, Wally, Frank, Capt. Shriver and myself take the necessary trip along Highway 101 to Hoquiam and then try to find a way to eventually reach Bremerton.. It was agreed by all that it was the largest city we noticed in our flyover that might still have enough infrastructure left to begin a rescue and rebuilding operation. It would be absolute chaos everywhere else around the region. We saw enough to know that. What we didn't really know was how bad it was before we even got to that destination. And by 2 p.m. we left the Lodge, with Wally sporting both his collapsible staff and sheathed wand.

It was to become a trip within the stark present and

sadly, give us too disturbingly, a preliminary view into the even starker future.

Traveling a rather steady 35-40 miles an hour, we arrived at the outskirts of Hoquiam in about an hour, and at that point it was clear that even Wally's road-clearing had its limits. The entire Olympic Peninsula was in shambles. River crossings, coastline and cliff-side roadways were blocked or impassable. For all we could see, we were the first to even attempt to make to make this trip or any venture beyond the rubble that had enveloped everyone. Only by having the assistance of citizens in and around Hoquiam were we able to construct a temporary bridge across the Hoquiam River at one of its narrowest sections just north of what used to be the town.

From there we had to travel back roads and almost pathways, partially cleared by Wally's staff/wand combination of trees and boulders. We eventually found the small village of Matlock and then took a side road up to Highway 101 on Road 102. From there we went north to Highway 106 to Belfair, backtracking on Highway 300 to Holly, Seabeck, Silverdale and then took Highway 16 into Bremerton. The drive took us two full days, with us sleeping in or around the truck at nightfall. This was the only route possible for us, and that was mainly because the Hood Canal at its lower end did not experience the surge of water that it had at its opening into the Sound itself. The Hood Canal Bridge was sunk in the combination of earthquake and flood that followed. However, the lower portion of the Canal suffered less overt destruction. But once we arrived in the metropolitan area of Bremerton/Silverdale, it was obvious big cities in this region were death traps.

And what was equally disturbing was the absolute

silence. There were no sirens, no wailing or calling out for help. There were only the raw signs of total annihilation… everywhere around us. Eventually… after winding our way through the debris-strewn roadways, we ended up in West Bremerton and found a clearing where survivors had begun erecting some very temporary shelters. This area, we later learned, was one of the only areas undamaged and clear enough to allow occupation. We were told it was the site of a housing project built for families during and immediately after World War II. It was called West Park. Fortunately for us survivors, it had recently been leveled to make way for some renewal project that never got off the ground due to lack of funding.

And it was here that we first got the news that things were far worse than my personal vision and our over-flight had led us to believe. Some residents of this emergency shelter had been able to set up a short-wave radio and were just finding out upon our arrival that this same destruction extended all the way down the West Coast, to and beyond the Mexican border.

From what could be ascertained, it seemed that the Cascadian Fault that buckled so violently in our area had unleashed the San Andreas Fault. In doing so, it forced the earth's plates adjacent to it to apparently shift northward. (see Appendix: **Earth's Tectonic Plates**) Cities, towns, bridges and roads throughout the coastal area of California were even more devastated than in this area. (see Appendix: **San Andreas Fault**).

All this came as a total shock to each of us. It was like what had happened in New Orleans during and after Hurricane Katrina was about to happen to the entire West Coast of America. And the national response was no doubt going to be the same… if not much worse. No one was to know where or how to begin anything. There was absolutely no intact infrastructure or trained personnel or proper facilities left intact to begin mounting a coordinated recovery process. And I was sure the aftereffects of this unparalleled disaster would continue far into the future.

Even at that earliest stage of attempting any rescue or recovery, Wally, Bernie and I began seeing what that first vision of mine had not anticipated. Maybe I was safe, but few others or little else around us was. There wouldn't be some bureaucratic expert fly in and analyze our situation and then make some headline-getting announcement that sure enough we had a disaster and that 'help was on its way'. We knew immediately there was not going to be a flyover, no headline-getting announcement nor any promise of help.

Seeing the smoke still rising from every direction in the city, Wally turned to Bernie and asked, "Where and how do we begin helping make things better, Bernie?"

And all Bernie could do was just shake her head in reply.

It was Frank and Capt. Shriver who overheard his question as they walked up to us and spoke almost in unison. "We begin in this place and do so by insuring that these people already here and any who arrive are safe and will be taken care of."

Frank then added, "We must set aside sections within this cleared area for different functions and then assign people to begin finding materials in the outlying areas to sustain them and us."

"Like what?" I couldn't help but interject.

It was then that Capt. Shriver answered. "We need areas for food and water distribution, for a medical facility of some sort, for an assembly area to allow for announcements and posting messages for loved ones and for a headquarters to coordinate all this. And I think each of us can help bring this about. From what I am seeing right now there is no coordinated effort taking place. And we have to begin immediately or even these survivors won't survive and much worse will soon ensue."

"What's that?!" I exclaimed, looking around *and thinking nothing worse could possibly happen.*

"Or total anarchy will inevitably result," he cautioned. "We need a group assigned to provide protection and insure some order as well. I have a suspicion that a breakdown is already beginning in the center of each of the major cities from Canada to Mexico. And as far as protecting us here, I think you, Wally, might be the perfect person to start insuring this. I've seen over and over what you and your staff and wand can do.

"Bernie, I need you to begin organizing all of us. Your ability to organize, implement change and establish order is unparalleled. Meanwhile, Frank and I will begin going from group to group of these huddled survivors and inform them what they can expect we will all begin doing. But we must hurry. Chaos and panic is inevitable if we don't."

"What about me? Is there something I can do?" I asked somewhat forlorn.

"Don't worry," Wally quickly replied. "You and I have our work cut out for us, once I see what I can do in this immediate area. We're going to need to spend time surveying the damage and its effects on everyone throughout this entire area. Just staying here is not going to address what is at hand. As hard as it is to say or even think, we have to 'Man Up', as I've heard others say. But I might also add that everyone needs to 'Man, Woman,

Animal and Bird Up'. There is no way I can pull off some magical stunt and make everything better. And sadly, I don't even have the slightest idea what 'better' may entail or mean anymore."

"Ok," I answered somberly. "I'll be ready whenever you say 'let's go'. In the meantime, maybe I can scout around the city here and see what I find."

And so it was for the next two weeks everyone worked feverishly to locate, organize and erect modest but safe shelters and other needed facilities. But the aftershocks were almost as terrifying as the actual, initial earthquake. Everyone's coping abilities were challenged to their limit.

In the meantime, as things settled into a shaky routine in our enclave, Capt. Shriver ventured forth with other members of various military and uniformed services that had found their way to our encampment and began a process of establishing a central command for all the services at what was left of the Bremerton Naval Shipyard's Headquarters. It was the closest facility to where we were staying, and it could provide some badly needed communication equipment and personnel.

It was from that point that coordination was begun with all the battered military facilities throughout the Western United States. From there, the surviving Marines at Oceanside and 29 Palms Bases and their equipment were dispatched; the same occurred from Naval bases at Everett, Whidbey Island, Bremerton and San Diego; and likewise from the Air Force bases at McCord, Fairchild and Beale; any Coast Guard units who survived and were available along the entire West Coast; and all Army units at Joint Base Lewis-McCord.

Also included in this group were all civilian law-enforcement personnel, be they city, county, state and federal that were located within this huge area. And the reason for this was that Martial Law was declared by order of the group of individuals that were assembled by Capt. Shriver. No one, not anyone, was depending on the leadership from Washington, D.C. Recent responses to other disasters, certainly far less in scope and devastation than this one, had taught everyone that.

In addition, Frank began to assemble various civilian leaders who held city, state and federal posts before the earthquake. And they began the thankless and nearly hopeless task of trying to prioritize the rescue, recovery and rebuilding process. And it was this group that began to notice the ever-widening political divisions that were developing beyond our mortally wounded, geological boundaries.

Just the same, it was Wally and I who were actually the first to really notice the evolving change. And it resulted from his having me go with him on those same over-flights that we performed before getting back to Willa's after the earthquake and tsunami. What we saw during those long flights was astonishing. As bad as the Northwest was pulverized by these two events, it was nothing compared to what happened once the San Andreas Fault was dislocated.

According to the National Geological Survey folks in Boulder, Colorado, who much later relayed this information to the Bremerton Naval Headquarters , the Cascadian buckling was so vast and extensive that it caused the northern portion of the San Andreas fault line to lunge forward over a quarter of a mile. (We later learned that the California Technical Institute facilities in Pasadena were totally destroyed and were unable to measure any of the events of that awful day.) And that buckling, in turn, initiated the displacement of all the spider-web-like fault lines extending off or adjacent to the San Andreas Fault. They all lifted, folded or buckled as well.

From the crest of the Cascade Mountains through that of the Sierra Mountains down to and including the San Bernardino Mountains and Wilderness Reserves to the Mexican border and over to the Pacific Ocean... all the earth's surface buckled, thrashed, heaved and broke-apart. What wasn't either on fire, under or swept away by water was leveled to unrecognizable rubble or now was impassable. There were very few desperate survivors left huddled in small enclaves. Looting was not yet organized in any way, but it and accompanying chaos were only days from beginning when Wally and I did our first, brief survey of the local area.

And upon seeing all this and after spending the next two weeks with Bernie and Wally doing whatever inconsequential tasks they asked of me , I later, upon our arrival back at the Quinault Lodge, summarized to Bernie what I felt and saw. It was to become the most prophetic and sobering words I have or will ever utter.

Capsulated, for anyone who should read this account after I am gone, there were three observations that I shared with her.

The first was that it very soon became clear that our nation was completely overwhelmed by the scope and extent of the losses that day on July 29th... so much so that you could almost sense a spiraling decay being set in motion. There was a palpable exhaustion of will, as well as resources. This catastrophe signaled the beginning of "The Disruption", which in turn began ushering what I have labeled the "Fracturization of America". The final *outcome of this would likely be seen much later.*

The second observation was that I could sense these two, side-by-side, overwhelmingly destructive events, occurring quite literally along our nation's entire western shoreline, convinced each of us who would live to tell about it that we, as a nation, no longer could be assured that we were the masters of our manifest destiny that we always assumed we were. Our future was no longer insured as a United States of Anything. What hundreds of years of settlement and progress had wrought, in one day had potentially been forever changed.

And third, and it could possibly have been my over-reacting to all that we have seen, the most startling change was to be one involving the fracturing and splitting apart of our collective and individual good will towards one another. It seemed to me there was an evolution towards an almost unconscious, tipping point. Everyone seemed to be drifting into being more rigid, more unyielding... more parochial. Most noticeable, it signaled a massive loss of confidence in ourselves and in our future.

THE SECOND VISION

SIX: "GOODIE"

Now that we were back at the Lodge, it gave me some time to review what was being done by others of our troop. Frank and Capt. Shriver were consumed in their respective capacities, trying to help organize and assemble the necessary personnel and equipment for recovery and rebuilding. All rescue work had ended by the time we left. Even if there were any trapped survivors, the need to try and save the growing number of refugees from starvation, exposure and thirst took precedence. And even help coming from countries overseas was not nearly enough due to the colossal breadth of damage and needs found everywhere. Diseases, resulting from loss of sanitary conditions and poor living conditions, were already beginning to take an added toll. Just before Bernie, Wally and I left for the Lodge; Frank admitted to me that the situation bordered on being hopeless. And this admission coming from ever-ready, ever-optimistic Frank caused me deep concern.

Once we got back to the rest of the Wagoners, we

found that the Lodge was full-to-overflowing with survivors stragling in from all over the western Peninsula. And like on the train ride from Chicago, all of us Wagoners had to bunk in one large room. I think it was a game room of some sort at one time. But it didn't matter. The three of us were so tired upon our return; we just fell immediately to sleep when Sophie showed us to our sleeping quarters. We didn't get up for the next twenty-two hours.

I was the first one to arouse and make my way out into the Lodge's main hall, the one with the massive fireplace. And no sooner had I shaken myself fully awake than Sophie approached me, announcing a most remarkable surprise.

"I have someone I want you to meet, Greg," she fairly purred. "Out of the blue, she showed up a few days ago. Unfortunately, she appears to have taken a blow to the head, because she has little memory of what has happened to her prior to coming here."

Figuring she was talking about somebody who would become a companion for Bernie or Wally, I showed little interest, yawned and stretched, with my front and rear paws arching my back and stomach, so that I looked like a suspension bridge. As I was doing so, peering from behind her was the most beautiful face of another Cattle Dog... one just like me, but of the female variety. I was stunned. And immediately, I lost all composure and sense of balance.

Stretching like I was at that moment, always took me some effort to do so correctly. Otherwise, I would stretch a little too much and pass a little gas. And wouldn't you know, I was so startled that this was exactly what happened. My moment of meeting the lady of my dreams was dashed by a painfully long, eerie-sounding chorus of staccato-like flatus. Everyone in that huge hall heard it and began to run, thinking it was a fire alarm of some kind. I could only manage another of my stupid smiles as I regained my usual, upright pose; that moment had to be the most embarrassing one of my entire life....

Unfazed by this, as was her custom by now with anything I did or said, Sophie went on to announce that the vision staring at me was named "Goodie". To me it fit perfectly. It was a name to be bestowed on someone who must usually reside in the loftiest of heavenly spheres. Of that I was sure. She had to be an absolute angel.

However, I need to correct or fully disclose a couple of issues that might cloud your impression of how this introduction and how my reactions proceeded from there. First off, while in the care of Howard back in Atlantic City, if I should dare characterize his concern for me so generously, he once took me to some animal clinic. Upon our arrival there, someone who must have just been bitten by something big and mean, came up to me in some back room with an intense look of wanting to get revenge. Both his facial expression and manner told me that even petting me was going to be painful. But to my shock and horror, he didn't approach my head. He went straight for my hind-end. And without any anesthetic, instructions, comments or 'howdy-do's', it felt like he must have placed a red-hot branding iron on my assorted privates in that area.

And in describing this moment, I probably should correct some misinformation I gave you sometime earlier. It was not when Howard gave me a bath that anyone knew that I could speak. No, it was the very instant the pain reached my then, but never after, ever-trusting brain; and I screamed,

"HEY YOU BACK THERE!! YEAH!! YOU WITH THE HOT POKER!!! GET AWAY FROM ME!!!! I'M NOT SOME FREE-RANGE CALF!!!!! TOUCH ME AGAIN THERE, AND I'LL TEAR YOUR ARM OFF!!!!!!"

Well, that caught both this wanna-be ranch hand and Howard completely by surprise, but not before any future, reproductive exploits of mine were to be the stuff of fiction. The deed had already been done. I was, as other "owners" of their "altered pets" so proudly and neatly proclaim: "fixed". Hence, I'm about as romantic as a hammer.

The second thing about me that may come as somewhat of a surprise is that I'm almost pathologically shy. Aside from Sophie and Bernie, forget Flo, Jennifer and Rita, who are just buddies, I am essentially speechless around those of the opposite sex. Let's face it, I'm just a dog. What's to be impressed by? I have fleas, scratch and pass gas. That's not exactly a combination or formula for having any engaging conversation or being able to foster an enticing, romantic interlude. And seeing this vision of beauty before me left me absolutely speechless and brought on a reflex urge to faint.

Sensing this, because she knew me like no one else, Sophie quickly spoke up. "Greg, aren't you going to introduce yourself to Goodie?"

Looking up at Sophie, as if she had just asked me to leap off the world's tallest building; I let out an almost inaudible whine and tried to clear my parched throat. It all made for a very pitiful introduction. Finally, as painful as it all appeared to everyone in that hall, I managed to mumble… "Hi, I'm Greg."

"And I'm Goodie, as you already know," this

heavenly apparition before me replied in sharp contrast to my fumbling. "Despite the loss of my memory for so much, after this terrifying earthquake, I do remember having heard so much about you. You are an absolute legend as I recall... here and everywhere. And it's so exciting to be here standing in front of you. And I've been worried sick that you'd be ok when you and the others were working over toward Seattle. It all must be so terrible. You're so brave. Would it be ok with you if we took a little walk outside and got better acquainted?"

By now, I figured she must have me confused with someone else, but anything would have been better than standing in front of everyone with my tongue hanging out and my becoming progressively and quite-possibly terminally mute.

"Sure," I answered, as I spun around without waiting for her to take the lead, like any gentleman might do, and scampered out the partially opened door into the large expanse of lawn behind the Lodge. And for the next hour, sitting on some beached driftwood in the shadow of the Lodge, in a state of pure rapture, I listened to her and wondered when I was going to have to wake up.

Something like this had never happened to me before. I'd always been a kind of joke or more often... invisible. Size does matter when you want to try to impress others. That puts two-legged folks and larger four-legged ones miles ahead of someone like me. If you constantly have to look down at someone, that doesn't give you many points in the world of influence, prestige or courtship. Especially if that someone is covered with bristly hair, drools occasionally and is prone to stare rather than talk.

But gradually I lost a measure of my reticence and over the next few hours I got to know more about Goodie, and I suppose she did of me as well. As best as I could understand, as the fog of my being overwhelmed at this initial encounter cleared, she did not come from these parts originally. How did I know? Her accent had more of a native, southern drawl. Just the same, upon retrospect, she never told me any substantive details about her life or her whereabouts prior to her being here at the Lodge. .

And I know... I know. You're probably thinking that talking dogs and cats is hard enough to grasp, but their also having some kind of regional accent is just too much to accept. But think of it. We have been listening to you coo and fuss over us animal kingdom folk for generations. Why shouldn't we end up sounding like we're from Alabama or Southside Boston once we could talk ourselves? It's only common sense. I'm sure, right now, if you found me in a smoke-filled room, playing a poker game with some gents in Camden, New Jersey, and heard them and me speak, we'd each one sound like blood-brothers. Just as I was sure on that late afternoon that my angel from heaven, Goodie, was originally from somewhere near Mobile, Alabama.

Even so, as I think about it now, her claim of losing her memory didn't seem to faze her nearly as much as it would have me. It was curious, but love is not just blind; it can make a fellow deaf as well.

But not Flo. She didn't say anything that day about my meeting Goodie nor on those that followed. But I could tell by her silence regarding Goodie that she had an entirely different impression of her. In fact, Flo never once talked about her to me. I just sensed her reserve and caution when Goodie would ever accompany me or when I spoke of her. If I think about it, I would probably say she was a little jealous of my happiness and of her being left out.

SEVEN: "THE DETERIORATION"

I have little memory of the next few days at the Lodge. I know that sounds selfish, given the unparalleled tragedy and resulting panic that befell all of us within that one hour we tried to picnic on that bluff overlooking the ocean. Goodie just seemed to stay beside me wherever I went, and my Wagoner companions shied away from us.

That period of indulgence ended when Wally came up to me about a week later and announced that he needed to have me follow him outside the Lodge... alone. Goodie appeared miffed by his asking this of me and looked at me like she thought I'd object. But when I saw the determination in Wally's manner, I knew his request had to be honored. To reinforce it, Flo quickly came up and almost herded me outside.

And now that I think about it that was about the last time I spent any time alone with Goodie. The urgency and pace of events that followed just seemed to keep us apart. I longed to be with her, but it was not to be. I frantically kept the hope alive that soon enough we'd be together again once this turmoil and upheaval had been met with the determination and will power necessary to begin anew.

Once outside the Lodge, Wally ordered me to sit and scratch that invisible collar with my left hind leg. And come to think of it, it wasn't until he did so that my realization of always having to wear it resurfaced.

Especially over the last week with Goodie, I had no inkling it was there, but as I thought about it, she seemed to study me when she or I were together. And her focus more often than not was not so much on my face but on my neck area.

I knew it was a silly thought, but it became even more puzzling when just before I sat down to do as Wally ordered, I turned and glanced toward the Lodge and there at one of the large windows was Goodie, staring at me without any apparent emotion. And her gaze seemed again directed at my neck again. It was not eye-to-eye.

Flo, noticing the exchange of looks, interrupted the process by adding, "Wally, I think it best if we head down past that clump of trees, away from the any peering eyes or curious onlookers. This process may take some time and we don't need to be interrupted."

"Good idea, Flo", Wally agreed. "More and more we need to be cautious about what Greg sees and how we choose to react to his visions. Maybe there are no more Emissaries to fight, but the aftermath of their influence and indoctrination, coupled with this transforming tragedy unfolding around us after the earthquake, there are other forces at work just as wicked and cunning. We should be more discreet and aware of our surroundings. And we must guard Greg, here, more deliberately."

"What, in particular, are you referring to when you say 'transforming tragedy'?" I then had to ask, hearing for the first time that I was about to be held in some kind of protective isolation.

It was Flo who answered my question and in a tone of voice that I had never heard her use before. It was filled with authority and insight. And it humbled me.

"For openers, it is now estimated that over four million people were killed initially in the earthquake and tsunami. And at least that number are estimated that will have succumbed in the days that have followed to now and undoubtedly even more will beyond today. Those injured, requiring major intervention are beyond counting. It is now estimated that the number of able-bodied individuals now residing in the Western portion of the country will be less than 200,000; and they are scattered far and wide, most of them in the less populated interior of the region. In the coastal areas alone, less than two percent of the population is healthy enough to exist at any functional level. But without their having clean water and food, that number is bound to decrease."

I was numbed by what she told me. I was so much so that I just followed Wally and Flo almost mindlessly to an area which was completely sheltered from anyone being able to see us from the Lodge or the lake. Once there, Wally again instructed me to sit and scratch the mysterious collar with my left hind leg. But this time he warned me, which I didn't recall he did the first time I did this immediately after the earthquake.

"Don't be frightened by what you see or hear in this vision", he began. "Although it is to be regional in nature, chances are I can intervene to help you avoid certain events or individuals which may have an impact either on you or us in some way. But keep in mind what you will experience or see might affect each of us personally in the future, whether it is immediate or in the weeks or months to come. Be prepared for some surprises and for some things that are only for me to try to understand. Now, hurry, we need to know what is ahead before we enter the next phase of this rebuilding process."

Hesitantly, I made a few vain attempts at scratching, but didn't touch my neck or that now-dreaded collar. Before I made actual contact with it, I did take one last look at both my colleagues, and what I saw was not encouraging. Each of them looked intensely worried... almost fearful. It was one of the most unsettling moments of my short life, which given the events we'd experienced together and the places we had traveled, this was not a hopeful sign.

What I began seeing initially was probably connected to the nearest event or circumstance that might affect me personally. And it was very encouraging at that. I saw myself staring at Goodie, with a look of all-absorbing love. At the same time, I even had a feeling of almost rapture. It was absolutely delightful. And it served to give me more confidence for what lay ahead for the region as a whole. It calmed me immediately.

Next, I began to see what was happening in other places outside our immediate neighborhood. Likely they were events or trends that were apparently going to impact our group, as well as countless others, at some time. The first one I later described as involving personal responsibility, the second one I thought amounted to a leadership crisis and the third appeared to reveal the advent of unsustainable promises.

First, I saw a bank building, somewhere in a very large city, and hanging on its street-facing, exterior wall was a gigantic banner, proclaiming a warning to all passersby. Someone standing nearby me read out loud what it said.

"ATTENTION EVERYONE!!!   30% of our country's population thinks it is ok to default on home mortgage loans. Think about this! Given that we have 300,000,000 people living in this land that means 105,000,000 of us could care less if the other 195,000,000 pick up the tab for their folly, poor judgment or misbehavior. The number of those who do not accept personal responsibility in acquiring the most basic of daily needs... shelter... means we as a people are at grave risk for an almost unavoidable economic collapse."

Then I saw inside the nation's Capitol Building, the White House and the Supreme Court Building and many of the other federal and state government office buildings with people rushing in and out of offices, up and down corridors, sitting in conference rooms or chatting in small clusters. It gave me the feeling I was watching a country club function; that everyone knew each other either socially, based on wealth or privilege or were being accorded deference due to belonging to a long standing, family-name dynasty. And rather than conducting needed business, there were only arguments, secrets being passed, plans being made for recreational jaunts or acquiring wealth through absolutely nothing constructive or decent.   These places, it was obvious, were devoid of true leadership; and the quality of representative government was being polluted beyond recognition.   Federalism and State governments, as they were meant to be, were now becoming a sham.   We, the people, animals, birds and trees of this land, were being duped and robbed.   It was as clear to see as if I was standing on the steps of one of the marble buildings at that moment.   And most importantly, this crisis in leadership was having an immediate effect on the regional response to our frightful losses and any recovery.

And lastly, my attention was drawn to seeing lines of people, in and about our region, waiting for help or service of some kind. They were lined up in front of government welfare offices, outside job recruitment centers or alongside countless medical facilities. And it appeared that the lines never moved. They were stationary. The system was frozen or paralyzed. From all indications the sweeping promises of security, entitlement and a safety net for all were empty. It appeared that most jobs were being shifted overseas in mass; excessive government spending was bankrupting the country and stopping any flow of relief funds out West to us; medical and social welfare facilities were closing or inoperable throughout our region. The contrast between this vision and the one of the nation and states' capitals, with all their hustle and bustle, unsustainable privileges and the resulting leadership crisis could not have been starker.

But no sooner than I had these three distinct visions, than another took their place. It was of a chalkboard. Across it scrolled words as fast as I could read them… which I can't or couldn't do before that particular vision.

I guessed it was part of Wally's magical vision-collar. I COULD NOW READ!! Or at least I could if I stayed in a trance state.

And on it began to appear what only could be described as descriptions or definitions of behavior… of the human kind. As bewildering as it was, I could only assume that later there might be more on this subject revealed to me… if there ever was going to be a third vision, associated with Wally's magical collar.

Then the chalkboard began streaming the following:

"Behavior is driven by actions, needs and desires for self-confidence, security and wisdom. And all of this unfolds in three, interactive arenas: within or to the individual; in response to the surrounding environment; and in relation to the immediate and historical timeframe in which individuals find themselves. Further, the merging of a person's lifetime and behavior is both predictable and unpredictable, given that it can be characterized as evolving in both a straight line, as in aging; and recurring, as in the normal transitional adjustments everyone must make throughout their lives. Behavior, in other words, is not static nor does it exist in isolation. And accompanying this process will naturally follow individual and collective belief systems; most commonly in the form of religious faiths.

"It's at that point, either on an individual level or through this collective process, remarkably good or devastatingly evil behaviors can arise. And for you personally, Greg, and for all others in this region who have just experienced this devastating, natural upheaval, this spiritual, intellectual and emotional process will ultimately determine your fate. Be alert, Greg. Be very alert."

And following this most disturbing vision there followed two more that were even more disturbing. Out of nowhere, Goodie appeared briefly. She was just staring at me unblinkingly and unflinchingly. It was the same look she had at the Lodge's window before I began this second vision session. She looked unfeeling and uncaring, and it was unnerving. And this was immediately followed with an image that seemed to depict my individual future. It was a void. There was no sense of feeling, knowing or awareness. It was simply filled with emptiness.

Out of shock and panic, I willed myself to awaken and vowed to avoid any more of this vision stuff if I could. It left me shaken and very disoriented.

To my additional shock, once I did regain something akin to consciousness and freedom from the dread of those visions, I found that I was lying in a tight curl and alongside me with her back touching mine was Flo. And kneeling over me and stroking me gently and reassuringly was my other best buddy, Wally.

"Take it easy, ole boy," Wally whispered soothingly. "Take it easy. Rest now. You've shared everything you've seen with us, as it unraveled before you. And I know it was shockingly disquieting. From this moment on you will never be left alone. Flo and I will always be by your side. I told you I'd protect you, and it's a promise the two of us will never break. Your fate is ours as well… for better or for worse. Now, just close your eyes and rest. We'll be right here."

"Always, old fella," Flo chimed in.

Exhausted and drained of all emotion, I laid my head back down and slept a dreamless sleep, as deep as the ones I used to enjoy on Howard's porch in Atlantic City.

THE THIRD VISION

EIGHT: THE WAGONER'S ASSIGNMENTS

The three of us finally arose and made our way back to the Lodge. Looking up as we climbed the natural rise to the native stone steps and wide porch, I again looked at the window next to the massive fireplace where Goodie had been staring at me before. Surprisingly, she was in the same spot, still staring. It was a bit unnerving, to say the least. Her focus and concentration didn't waver, and there was little-to-no warmth in her facial expression. And as I looked over at Flo and Wally, they both nodded their heads as if to acknowledge what I was seeing. It was all so strange, my just coming from having the disturbing visions and now seeing this vacant, yet intense, stare.

But once inside the Lodge, Sophie came up to us, announcing in a most excited voice, "You three need to go into the gift shop area where some of the Lodge's employees and a few local neighbors have set up a shortwave radio, which can both send and receive messages. What they are hearing is astonishing. None of us had any idea what this catastrophe was to bring... to so very many. Hurry, go and hear the developing news."

With Wally leading the way, the three of us eventually squeezed into the converted Lodge's, gift shop and positioned ourselves on an empty window ledge seat. The room was packed and totally silent, except for the static-interrupted voice of a BBC announcer. And for the next hour we all stood or sat spell-bound at what we heard.

Throughout the announcer's reporting there were updates and long pauses as it appeared the news staff was trying to sort out what was verifiable and what was still rumor. To summarize as best I can, he was describing a series of events that were all but erasing any habitable living areas everywhere throughout the Pacific Rim. There wasn't just one giant tsunami. There were two. And the second one, caused by the buckling and advancing of the San Andreas Fault was twice the size of the one caused by the Cascadian Fault buckle. They occurred one hour apart. And it was being estimated that the second tsunami reached a height of over three hundred feet!

Most islands in the Pacific were almost completely inundated. Coastline cities were in shambles, suffering an equally massive loss of life as had been witnessed here on the mainland. Hawaii and Alaska had to be evacuated. There was no way to supply them, given the damage to their respective states and the infrastructure loss here on the mainland. All American troops and any removable materials stationed overseas, whether in the Pacific, Asia and Europe or elsewhere were ordered to return home. Cruise ships within the Atlantic Ocean, Mediterranean and Caribbean Seas and any which survived in the Pacific Ocean were commandeered to help evacuate islands and coastal areas. They, along with U.S. Naval ships, were ordered to bring U.S. citizens, who had survived, back to

Gulf or Atlantic ports for repatriation.

And because there were no ports left along the entire U.S. Pacific coastline, and only temporary docks could be constructed as time and material would allow, the bulk of the nation's fleets had to seek refuge elsewhere along the remaining U.S. coastal ports. The western portion of the U.S. was inaccessible by sea.

But then there were the staggering problems being discovered just inland, particularly in what used to be California. The magnitude of their earthquake destroyed the Colorado River and San Joaquin Valley aqueducts and canals. Both agriculture and drinking water sources were gone for most of its citizens.

And not to be outdone, the tragedy of all this struck the Sacramento Delta as well. The earthquake and the resulting tsunami either liquefied or destroyed their levees, allowing the water surging in from the ocean into the San Francisco Bay to sweep up the Sacramento River and force salt water over countless acres of farmland and the surrounding farms, towns and cities.

In less than an hour, much of California had been turned back into a stark, desert environment... almost totally arid and without potable water; it was now either flooded or decimated. The jewel of 20th Century ingenuity and commerce was no more. Any and all survivors along the coastal region were being asked to assemble at designated sites for immediate evacuation. Where possible, those survivors in the northern part of the state that needed to be moved were to be quartered in areas from Chico to the State's border with Oregon. But many had to be ferried on into Nevada and Oregon for safety and shelter. Those in the southern part of the State were being bused and trucked in over-packed vehicles of all sizes and shapes along makeshift roadways, around collapsed bridges and viaducts to Arizona and all points east. From all the descriptions we were hearing on the Lodge's shortwave, it seemed like the 1930's Depression Era migration to California was now beginning anew... in reverse. The one bright note in all this indescribable destruction was that Boulder Dam had been unaffected by the earthquake.

Engineers, civil authorities and what few civilian and military leaders were left in the region soon began planning some framework for rebuilding new but vastly smaller communities in the region. But even they knew from the outset that what had happened to California and the entire West Coast meant that these States and the entire country was never going to be the same.

Listening to this for that hour put Wally, Flo and I into a muted state of shock. We knew the damage had to be severe, but we never imagined the global extent of it all. Afterward, each of us went back to our common sleeping room and collapsed.

The next day Bernie and Wally called us Wagoners together, along with all of Sophie and Frank's extended family and Stella. We met in the shortwave radio room, which allowed them to coordinate communication with Frank and Capt. Shriver who were still in the Bremerton area. Purposefully left out of the group was Goodie... at Wally's urging. And that puzzled me.

During the course of that meeting, it was decided that Frank, Capt. Shriver and Happy needed to return to the Lodge as soon as possible. Both the desperate nature of what they were having to cope with and the visions that I had about what was potentially or actually taking place required that everyone meet and discuss what should be done next.

Wally described the situation in the most elementary of terms; this country was now facing a "Humpty Dumpty" moment, in which neither all the "kings horses and men" nor the previous will and might of this once mighty nation could put all the pieces of this broken land back together again. And most certainly it could not be done with the once-thought-of impenetrable and break-proof, protective shell it once had. Even more disturbing, as he ventured further into the ramifications of what was evolving, demonstrating that his wisdom and understanding as a full blown wizard had achieved almost Walt-like strength and insight, he confided to our group that this unraveling of will and determination extended from the highest civilian levels. A tipping point had been reached. We in the West were essentially being abandoned. To anticipate or look at the future in any other way, he summarized, would only delay whatever recovery process had to be formulated and instituted.

It was shocking to hear him talk like this. But, being the resourceful and stalwart gentlemen they were, Frank and Capt. Shriver agreed to return immediately and begin a review and develop some plan for our moving forward. They thought they could arrange for a helicopter from Joint Base Lewis-McCord to ferry them back to the Lodge. Capt. Shriver said to expect them to be back by the next afternoon.

And sure enough about 2 p.m. the next day there was a loud clattering sound approaching us from the lake and before we could gather our wits and calm ourselves that we were not about to experience another aftershock or earthquake, Frank and Capt. Shriver's helicopter landed on a fairly level portion of the Lodge's lawn. As soon as they exited the craft, it took off again, because as we learned later, the crew wanted to be back at their home base before nightfall. There were no exterior lights anywhere, except in absolute emergencies.

Immediately, after the two travelers hugged and greeted their family members and the rest of us Wagoners, they called for a general meeting. It was all too evident that they were now completely driven by attempting to help coordinate and assist in managing the impossible task of rebuilding this shell of a region. And as we were soon to learn... we had to do so without the help of any outside resources. The Western half of the United States was on its own.

It was Frank who spoke first. He limited his presentation to what was being done at the local levels around the Northwest. Capt. Shriver was to describe what was being done on a more region-wide scale. And to start with, Frank shocked us with the announcement that everywhere was now under Martial Law... even us here at the Lodge. All decisions were now being made at a central location at the West Park compound and at the usable portion of the Naval Headquarters at the shipyard in Bremerton. Whatever civilian and military authorities and commanders there were who had survived in the region have been ordered to report to these two areas. The civilian leaders came to West Park, and the military ones went to the shipyard facility. But the two did not operate independently. All final decisions were made jointly.

"I'm afraid I don't have much encouraging news for you this afternoon," he began. "And to be as brief as possible, given that all of us are so exhausted and our attention spans are understandably limited, let me outline what had to be done for any potential, long-term survival for any of us in this immediate area.

"We have had to begin evacuating everyone from any metropolitan area. There is too much destruction in them to ensure safety and sanitary conditions. And we have had to limit the number of people who will occupy any of these newly forming communities. These communities are now starting to be built in outlying areas. And where any clearing and ground preparation is needed, the members of that community have to do it. We have designated that only 2,500 people are allowed in any one of them. To allow any more would make it too difficult for them to provide for their own survival.

"They are essentially on their own. We have broken down the number of their assigned duties to five, and each is a mandatory assignment. Each of the five groups is to consist of five hundred people; the number anticipated and necessary, we hope, to accomplish their goals. The five assignments are to: provide adequate living shelter for themselves; plant, harvest, scavenge for food and drill for water; construct sanitation and sewer networks; secure the necessary building materials and equipment for the other assignments to be determined at a later date, some of which would most likely be quite rudimentary; and clear and prepare the land, build roadways and the necessary buildings for the community's ability to function. There is to be no schooling for at least one year. Everyone possible will be assigned some task. And for obvious reasons, except for those women already pregnant, further child bearing for this first year is highly discouraged. Newborns may be the hope for a new life, but in order to have any life, this next year will require austerity, sacrifice and restraint.

"All of us recognize the elementary needs and urges for comfort and privacy. Topping that list for the foreseeable future, however, has to be our ultimate survival. And Capt. Shriver will explain why that is now. 'Phil', I guess it's your turn."

Getting up slowly, as Frank squeezed in between Sophie and me on one of the overstuffed chairs in the Lodge's great hall, Capt. Shriver cleared his throat and drank from a coffee mug that Stella had given him after he just entered the room, and they had had a long embrace.

And maybe here I should add that Happy also returned with them on their flight. Interestingly, Goodie made a beeline over to him when he finally settled down in front of the Shriver's. And as she did so, she made a conscious effort to look over at me, as if to say, "See, loser. Here's a real hero." If it hadn't been for the intensity of what Frank and now Capt. Shriver were saying, I would have been crushed, but Flo who was sitting beside me bumped her head against my shoulder, as if to say, "Never mind. Stay focused." Then Capt. Shriver spoke.

"Well, folks, as Frank has alluded to, I will be speaking about the military response to what is now happening, and describe to you as best as I can the conditions that exist beyond our immediate area, particularly those found in California and in our nation's capital. Sadly, my report is not encouraging.

"Our federal government is essentially collapsing. Whatever communication we have from them or to them is uncertain and qualified, and often it is by or to someone who is far down any link of a valid chain of command. Like with Rome, there seems to be a lot of fiddle-playing, while much of the western half of their realm has being sacked. In our case it was not by invading armies, but by an indifferent, but perfectly orchestrated, natural event. Someone witnessing what has happened to one half of the world from beyond earth would say that we have been participants in an awesome and grand spectacle: the almost unimaginable, hemispheric shifting of tectonic plates, which override a swirling, fiery planetary core. This shifting, uplifting and the massive series of waves that followed are but a hiccup in a Universe in which stars implode and explode as massive supernova and in which galaxies collide. If there was ever an example of how the natural world behaves on a frightfully grand scale, this was it. Wherever in this Universe conscious beings exist, we will be reminded from time to time that this is to be expected. The only option we have is to try and accept, adjust and rebuild. This indifference will never change. It is the order of things.

"But you might say, 'There must be a balance to all this mindless destruction'. Or ask 'How do we find peace and comfort in spite of what has or will occur again and again?' or 'Where can we turn?' I'm not the one who should speak to or answer these questions. Maybe there is someone amongst you who can or will some day. However, right now it is time to begin anew, in the midst of our grief and the unbelievable destruction... despite puzzling and ever-mounting, unacceptable attitudes and behaviors that have resulted in our getting minimal help from any outside agency or government. We must consider that we are basically alone in our response to this disaster. And again, some day, someone else will have to explain why that is.

"I preface what I am now about to say with these previous remarks because I have been swamped constantly by these issues and questions. And with you, my wife and assembled dear friends, I want to be as candid and forthright as possible before I explain what has been happening with the areas of my responsibility in this rebuilding process.

"On a local level, we have begun developing sites for specialized medical facilities, which are rudimentary at best. No longer will we have so-called 'general' hospitals. We cannot afford the duplication that having these entails. There will only be four specialty hospitals in our region. They will be for the disciplines of orthopedics; neurology; infectious diseases and internal medicine, which will include the specialties of pulmonary, cardiology, gastroenterology, urology, etc. Both adults and children will be admitted to these facilities. There will not be any stand alone, children's hospital. They will be staffed by any of the doctors and surgeons who have survived. In the small communities that Frank mentioned being organized, there will only be non-physician personnel providing the care, such as nurse practitioners, physician assistants and emergency medical technicians.

"All security will be provided by our own personnel. As was mentioned, we are no longer under civil administration. Martial Law has been ordered and all local government and civilian officers have been sworn into the military for the time being. They, and the troops left in our various, regional installations are now being stationed in and around our soon-to-be, thirty-odd, rebuilding sites.

"And we have begun clearing out all major metropolitan areas of any survivors. Evacuation of needed supplies and material from these areas will be done by our forces, as will any demolition and plans for rebuilding. And frankly, given what I am about to tell you, any rebuilding in these destroyed metropolitan areas will be years away from now.

"To provide for any subsequent return of electrical

power, we have conscripted all remaining power company employees. And I might add right now that each of you in this room is subject to conscription at a moment's notice. Demand and need will dictate when that happens. We have done the same for any well-drilling operators and the surviving remnants of drilling companies. Our hope is to begin drilling for water at each of the evacuation sites as soon as possible. Farmers and ranchers in the less damaged outlying areas have also been drafted into service. Without their help, no one's survival is likely in this region. All agricultural products grown in this region will be kept here. There will be no exporting. If there is, it will only be when our stores are full to guarantee our survival through the upcoming winter months. Any exportation will have to be paid for in advance by the importing, government authority. No international business is to be conducted on a private basis for the time being.

"And on that note, we are issuing script for money. We are now doing all business or personal transactions on an 'I.O.U.' basis. So completely has been the lack of federal response that we have had to take the extreme act of issuing our own equivalent of currency... in the form of script.

"A central command or government headquarters, if you will, is now being debated as to its ultimate location. And because of the massive disruption to the continuation of any functional society in most of the coastline cities of California, we are hoping to set it up adjacent to the Joint Base Lewis-McCord, outside Tacoma. But for now, most of the assembled authorities or any regional planning is being conducted from the Naval Headquarters in Bremerton's Naval Shipyard. The Naval Base in Everett was completely destroyed in the earthquake and by its resulting tsunami. The waves were still fifty-to-seventy-five feet high when they hit that area head-on. A couple of the support-group vessels were even swept up into the city proper.

"So, saying all this, where does that leave all of you here?   What roles are you to play in this rebuilding process?   Frank and I have been discussing this for the last week, and he asked me to inform you what your roles are to be.   Unfortunately, I have to advise you that what I am about to say is a departure from the traditional operational mode that each of you have been accustomed to using. You will no longer be working as a unit. The Wagoners will be broken up, separated by both assignment and location, with some of you being sent far away from the others."

This was followed by a collective, audible groan with each of us casting almost frantic looks of surprise at him and at one another. Our strength and purpose had been welded by our unity. We were sure of that after all we'd seen and done. To separate us amounted to siphoning off that energy and will. It came as a shock, and both Frank and Capt. Shriver anticipated that it would stun us.

"Let me pause here a moment," Capt. Shriver continued, well aware of the flood of objections that would soon come. "Just like the lives of millions and millions of people and any other conscious beings outside this Lodge, scattered near and far, having experienced immeasurable loss, unimaginable dislocation and the inconceivable reality of living under martial law with total strangers, it now becomes your turn to share in their anguish and insecurity of what lies ahead. No one can escape it. And no one can anticipate nor imagine what the long term effects all this upheaval is going to have on our attitudes, behaviors and the decisions arising from them. Frank and I can only hope and pray that sometime in the not-too-distant future we will all be reunited. It's a time I find myself dreaming about. But, honestly, at this moment, it seems so very far away.

"So, with our sincerest apologies, I must proceed with the assignments for each of you. And first off, I want to begin with Jennifer and Rita. The two of you will have the responsibility of traveling throughout the Puget Sound area, canvassing and recruiting any of your fellow species and the trees for whoever can be scouts and patrol members. We need you to lay out a grid of the region and then find others of your kind that can locate pockets of food and fresh water resources, be they berries, mushrooms, nuts, orchards, nurseries, untended commercial gardens, recently active or potential agricultural zones and clear streamlets for drinking water.

"In addition we need you to organize others of your kind both to patrol the streets and skies to alert our headquarters if there is any looting or other criminal mischief taking place. We just don't have the personnel available to patrol all the vast area now left uninhabited but still filled with materials we can eventually use. Following the earthquake, fires have consumed much of the downtowns; but there are still many neighborhoods with usable materials that could eventually be of value in our rebuilding somewhere else. You and your colleagues are to become our eyes and ears on the ground. And we'll need you to begin right away. Both of you will go back with Frank and I tomorrow… as will others of you when I have given you your assignments.

"Sophie and Bernie will be responsible for overseeing and reporting on the settlements from both sides of the Columbia River up to and including Biggs and then northward to the Canadian border, using roughly the eastern foothills of the Cascade Mountains as your eastern boundary. You do not need to be concerned about the Portland metropolitan area and the other cities and communities to the south; they will be someone else's responsibility.

"You two will report to Frank, and he will arrange any transportation that you will need. Unfortunately, the roads are not easily passable for much of the area you will be working in. And again, Frank will help you with water or air transportation when it is necessary. Your careful observation, supervision and chronicling of the settlements will be crucial for any successful recovery and rebuilding. Both of you have the temperament and perseverance, as it has been well documented in your travels across this country and then around the world, to do this assignment ably. I am optimistic that as devastated and broken as the psyches and bodies of our regional neighbors are, you can still help them begin anew. And throughout your journeys and contacts with anyone you work with or talk to, I need you both to monitor the behavior patterns of all survivors. Keep a journal if necessary. And then report your findings as well to Frank and myself.

"Happy and Goodie, our newest member of this group, will accompany Frank and I back to Bremerton as well. Once there, they will begin a survey and recruitment of all the other animals in the region to provide additional protection and prevent looting. It is important that packs of various animals do not get organized. The chaos that has been created by this disaster provides a perfect opportunity for stray animals to form dangerous mobs.

"You two will need to negotiate and coerce, as necessary, to enlist others in helping to rebuild. And on that note, Frank and I have begun discussing the need to develop some sort of participatory role that animals, birds and trees will play in the formation of a new government. It most likely will not be one vote for each individual. A more reasonable option would likely be something like a block vote, based on some to-be-determined collective number. Assure each participant you talk to that their voice will be heard. We have to avoid the many mistakes of the past as much as possible. And we need all the help we can get from everyone and everything.

"Both of you will report to me. And I know that Goodie is new to this group. We welcome you, despite the desperate times that we now face. Would you like to say anything to us before I go on?"

And to my amazement, she did nod her head that she wanted to.

"It will be such a privilege and honor for me to work with you and the Wagoners. I have followed your accomplishments with keen interest and admiration. Thank you for giving me this opportunity to help."

And then again she made it a point to cast a curious look at me, as if to say that she had other reasons in mind as well. It was just too confusing for me. My feelings for her were so powerful and all-consuming that I couldn't sort out what was happening between us. I only hoped that one day she and I would be together again on some joint assignment. I was smitten by her, and my heart raced just thinking about that possibility.

Interrupting my reverie, Capt. Shriver then turned to the three of us huddled together.

"As for Wally, Flo and Greg, it is to be their unenviable task to spend the next weeks or possibly even months working with and assessing the situation throughout most of Oregon and all of California. But the majority of your time should be spent in California. Their needs are epic, and their resources are scant... as will be any outside assistance. It is on those citizens that the greatest burden of this societal collapse will fall. You are to do whatever you can to protect and assist them in their recovery process. And like Bernie and Sophie, I need you three to monitor closely the attitudes and reactions of those you encounter and live amongst. More than the paltry response from the federal government and the rest of the country's citizens, it will be the will and determination of the people who you work with that will make the difference in whether they survive this onslaught of nature's fury. Their attitudes will no doubt determine the eventual outcome of what happened to them on July 29th.

"Finally, for Jimmy, his family and the others of Frank and Sophie's family and Stella, my most faithful and loving, lifetime companion, Frank and I would ask that you folks stay here and continue the work that has already begun to form the one community of 2,500 here on the Peninsula. It will no doubt be the only one on the entire Puget Sound Peninsula, given the massive destruction and loss of life over its entire length and breadth. Through your shortwave radio, you need to communicate your presence and intentions to rebuild here at this site. And of course, you'll use this Lodge as your headquarters and as the seat of local government.

"And that should about sum up all that I have to say. Are there any questions?"

And again to my surprise, there were none. It was as if each of us knew that what we felt and saw occurring that day on the bluff overlooking the Pacific Ocean was going to change our lives completely. It was the beginning of a tragedy that would seem to have no end for each of us and for this country. Looking at Flo and Wally, I sensed they were experiencing the same emotions as I. This was our last day to be the intact Wagoners, all assembled in one place. Everyone could feel it.

NINE: THE WAGONERS'S RESPONSE

From the reports that Wally and I got from Bernie, but less often from Sophie, over the next three months, I want to briefly outline what we've learned so far as to how the other Wagoners were faring during our prolonged separation.

Probably of all the Wagoners, it was Jennifer who I was proudest of and was the most stunned to learn about what role she played in providing needed safety and protection for the survivors of July 29th.

No sooner had Frank arranged for her transportation to Seattle from Bremerton, than she set out on her own, bidding Rita a fond good-bye and began her recruiting.

When possible, she would hitch rides on military vehicles passing by. And believe me, it had not been that long since dogs, cats and your various, other household pets and pests could express themselves coherently and forcefully. It still caught everyone by surprise when she called out. Dressed in her usual stylish manner, despite the ravages seen everywhere, she would arch her back and yell out at a slowing Army or Marine convoy, "**NEED A RIDE HERE**!!!... AND THERE IS NO TIME TO WASTE!!!

Often she would push a large cardboard box over to a nearby curb and stand fully erect on top of it. Both her insistence and ingenuity got her rides on whatever was the first group of vehicles passing by.

And so it went, with her eventually covering over 7,500 square miles from the traditional uppermost snowline of the western Cascade mountains to the Puget Sound, from Bellingham to Olympia, she recruited both the domesticated animal life and those who customarily resided in the wilds for her assignment. From the lowlands there were horses, cows, goats, sheep and beavers; and from the highlands there were bears, bobcats, cougars, deer and elk. And each in turn spoke to others of their ilk until there was literally an army of stealthy and visible scouts and enforcers roaming and patrolling throughout the region.

Obviously, the bigger the creature, the louder the voice and the more weight and authority it led to addressing someone who was about to or in the midst of committing an infraction. Nothing inhibits the urge to "step-toe" or prowl the massive number of empty streets, looking for contraband or creating mischief than coming face-to-face with a patrol, comprised of a grizzly, cougar and two rangy bobcats. Soon looting and other criminal activities became far too risky for even the most hardened perpetrator.

Jennifer had established a huge and visible network of neighborhood watches and protectors, through her astonishing and up-to-then-unknown organizational and managing skills, ones none of us knew she had. Her engagement in this assignment became an obsession. It was an overnight wonder. I was eager to see and congratulate her as soon as our own assignment was completed.

Likewise, Rita literally lofted herself into the annals

of permanent historical records that were surely to follow this terrible time and staggering rebuilding process. From her withdrawn, often sarcastic and jaded view of the world and its inhabitants, she took Capt. Shriver's charge and became obsessed with insuring a future for the new communities being established throughout the region.

Not needing anyone to transport her, and given her limitless physical strength, stunningly beautiful appearance and markings, consisting of a brilliantly white head and body, heightened by a sparkling yellow crest... all unlike any other native bird for thousands of miles in any direction... gave her instant recognition and unlimited access to anywhere in the region. When she flew into a roosting flock of birds in the area, there was an immediate and attentive silence.

And within days of getting her orders, she had begun recruiting eagles, ospreys, Canadian geese, assorted varieties of ducks, pigeons and countless gulls to become the ears and eyes of the devastated Puget Sound region. Ostensibly, as Capt. Shriver had outlined to her, they were to scout for food and fresh water sources, but quickly these ever-present eyes-in-the-sky became first responders to the newly forming communities' needs and inevitable emergencies. Her stalwart band had a steely purpose in all they did. Their discipline was remarkable. Over time, hundreds of lives were to be saved... directly or indirectly.

Rita was a true hero to all. She was no longer the hawker who used to perch on the railing of Steel Pier in Atlantic City. Just hearing all this about her made me proud to have been associated with her the time I was. But, again, like with Jennifer, I had the sense that time, distance and future events might forever keep us apart.

Sophie, on the other hand, was not doing as well as

any of us expected or hoped, at least not according to what little information I could get from Bernie. She was no longer communicating directly with either Wally or I.

Frank oversaw her labors and travels, as you would expect. But even that relatively close monitoring by him, given the desperate nature of what all of us were consumed by, was not providing enough support and comfort to one of my dearest friends.

Given that her assignment was to travel to each of the communities being organized over the vast area from the Columbia River to the Canadian border, from the crest of the Cascade Mountains to the Pacific Ocean, it was no wonder that she was becoming more exhausted. Fortunately, early on, it was decided that she need a fulltime driver and a vehicle devoted just to her. And Frank went along with her from time to time for support and company.

And certainly her mild and welcoming manner allowed her to move freely and easily amongst all the survivors in these newly evolving villages. *I imagined there was no issue too private that others would not discuss with her.* She was the perfect choice to monitor any serious change or disturbing behaviors that were becoming too common throughout this land and could lead to a crisis. She mingles easily within any group or setting and always has a sympathetic ear for whatever she is being told. *If it were possible, I think she should be crowned Queen of the Northwest.*

My assumption is that whenever she notices any attitudes or signals that could be signs of disruption for the rebuilding process that she will report them both to Bernie and to Frank. But my own sense of her is that she is internalizing what she is seeing and what has happened to this area and is now becoming physically and emotionally exhausted. She misses being with Frank and with not seeing her family at the Lodge. My real concern is that too much has been asked of her. Even now, Wally tells me there is a melancholy in her voice and manner, whenever he hears from her or on the odd moments that he can see her, when he is called back to Tacoma or Bremerton to see Capt. Shriver or Frank.

I fear the youthful vigor and optimism of my dear Sophie is being swept away just like so many lives were on that awful day in July. And even for a dog, possibly much to your surprise, it breaks my heart to realize this is happening to her. Even more than Goodie, I so love my Sophie. Despite all the trauma and chaos that is and has happened around us, I believe she knows that. And in these trying times that gives me some comfort.

Still, acknowledging that, I do wish I could get in touch with Goodie. I worry about her as well. And I dearly wish I could get some time off to be with her. All this "puppy love" business is new to me, particularly at the mature age that I have now reached. I think of her constantly. In truth, I'm infatuated with her. I just hope she feels the same about me. It will be so wonderful to see her again. I daydream of her whenever I am not preoccupied with whatever Flo and Wally want me to do... sigh...

Anyway, that leads me to report on what Bernie has been doing over these last three months since Capt. Shriver sent us off on our various assignments. The primary source of any news I got about Bernie was through Wally. They seemed to communicate by way of some wizard-like ether that totally defies any comprehension. And it was clear that Wally was becoming progressively more concerned about her as well. According to him, she seemed more and more consumed by the assignment given to her by Capt. Shriver. It was as if her normal Herald duties, along with now having to chronicle, report and organize, were overwhelming her: that and something more. The way he explained it to me, it was like she was having premonitions of some kind. It was like she was not just exhausted from being duty-bound; but that there was a dread of an impending loss, even more personal and devastating than that which surrounded all of us day-by-day.

He said these premonitions she was having were not concrete or specific, but they were becoming more intense as the days and weeks passed since we were last together at the Lodge. He went on to say that while both she and he had progressively gained more insight and strength since our first becoming Wagoners, there seemed to be an ominous, even regressive, limit or decline overshadowing their abilities and insights.   It was like a mental or perceptual fog, possibly arising from recent events and all their travels. He was concerned it was hampering both of their remarkable skills and their having the comforting assurance of the safety and necessary foresight for us all.

I tried to get Wally to tell me if there was anything more specific as to what Bernie was sensing, but he appeared non-committal... even evasive to my persistent questioning. This worried me even more. I sensed he knew more than he was telling me, even more than he was willing to share with his sister.   There was a shadow drifting across all our relationships. It was not stemming from a lack of trust, being overworked or experiencing too much calamity and tragedy. It was of an indeterminable threat, one that was so sinister and effective that each of us appeared powerless to fend it off. And all this unnerved me so much I kept myself constantly at Wally's heels, almost touching him with each step he took. He would look down at me occasionally with a sincere but unspoken expression of awareness. He knew I sensed something undeniably dangerous was lurking in our midst.

And yet, Bernie went about her duties of overseeing and reporting on the newly developing communities, extending from the Portland area to the Canadian border. And from all that we heard, they were slowly but steadily gaining materials and skills to sustain themselves for the bad weather to come. And it was all due to the efforts of each of us in this region. There was essentially no help from the federal level. As I was later to learn, the extent of this disaster and the stalemate that had been developing through the years in Washington, D.C. had now created a total roadblock.

Maybe fires consumed Rome when that empire fell, but it was a bureaucratic and leaderless log jam that appeared finally to be bringing our government to its knees. The reasons why and the ramifications of it all were soon to be revealed to me.

But Bernie soldiered on, making notes, giving reports and encouraging everyone to be strong and brave. Her intrepid manner was an inspiration to the fifteen or so new settlement communities trying to be developed and survive in the area.

Happy, on the other hand, was merrily going about his business on the western side of the Puget Sound. From all I could find out, it seemed he was patterning his efforts after those of Jennifer by enlisting all the various four-legged creatures he could find to help with any community building. Unfortunately, the resources were fewer on that side of the Sound, so the impact of what he was attempting did not have the force that Jennifer's efforts had.

But, give the guy a break! He was at least trying and not being an overblown egomaniac, like he was onboard the ships and whenever he was in a new situation. His insecurities seem to have lessened, and most importantly of all, he, too, was in love... with MY GOODIE!! From all I could glean, they were inseparable, which made my life even more miserable. I wanted so badly to get back to that area and try to win my love back. But Flo and Wally would have none of it. They seemed to sense something that I couldn't or didn't. They would always quickly change the subject whenever I mentioned her name. She was dismissed quickly from any conversation. That, of course, left me even more despondent. Happy with Goodie was not a good combination for keeping up my morale.

And both he and Goodie reported to Capt. Shriver on a very regular basis; more so than anyone else in our band. They seemed to take advantage of their close proximity to his headquarters and made sure he was aware of any progress they made. That, in turn, gave them more and more access to the inner workings of the rebuilding process and most importantly, to our time off and whereabouts.

So much so, that after the first couple of months, it was being observed that the two of them were not seen in that section of the Puget Sound as often. They appeared to be traveling incognito to other parts of the region... or beyond. And Happy, if anything, according to what Flo and Wally sensed, was being completely duped by Goodie. She had been and apparently was still manipulating him for her own purposes... whatever they might be.

It was a deepening mystery to everyone but me. All

I wanted was to see her. Forget the intrigue. And I waited impatiently for the day I might get some word directly from her. And then one day, about four weeks later, I did. It was a glorious moment.

And that leads me to Frank and Capt. Shriver's tireless efforts. On the one hand, Capt. Shriver's responsibilities progressively diminished in the overall rebuilding effort due to the presence of a tattered but still significantly intact military presence in the area. And this only became more so as the sailors and troops returned home from being recalled. Within two months of the disasters, there were no uniformed personnel stationed overseas. They had all deployed back home to the States. And even though Martial Law was still in effect for all this time and probably would be for at least three to six more months, by everyone's estimation, the civilian population did not mind. And this, if for no other reason, spoke to the quality of leadership and dedication of all our military forces.

Certainly, the bravery and composure of any soldier, marine, airman or sailor is tested in combat to the most extreme, but equally telling is how they react in a setting of total destruction and possible chaos of a society. It would be so easy for anyone in their positions to become autocratic or dictatorial and terrorize the populace. But the one remarkable, to me even lovely, outcome of all the mayhem and destruction of those months after July 29th, was the universal cooperation and humanity shown at all levels by the men and women in uniform to the civilian population in everyone's attempts to restore some form of self-government.

And Capt. Shriver stood tall in that initial phase. He stayed primarily in the Bremerton Naval Headquarters, coordinating us Wagoners and the settlements being organized on the western portion of Puget Sound. Frank, on the other hand, directed his focus on the eastern side.

And it was clear to me that as Sophie became progressively more fatigued and emotionally drained, Frank lovingly slipped beside her to bolster and relieve her of most of her duties. He was, in all respects, a very competent individual. I sensed this from the first day we met, even as he scolded me after my initial, joyful outburst riding in the back of his old pickup truck. He is a prime example of the innate leadership qualities that are so remarkable in a civilian population that is allowed to be free, but knows it must attain a firm maturity and sense of self to succeed and prosper. He, in all our travels and perils, never became abusive or short-tempered. He would react with a calmness and thoughtfulness that served as the backbone of our little troop. And now, in the mire of what was left after these terrible natural events, he continually assumed more and more responsibilities. And one of his most important, at least to him, was to take Sophie under his wing.

The two of them kept in close contact with their family members back at the Lodge through the shortwave radio connection in each of the newly evolving communities. And after a couple of months following our leaving the Lodge, he and Sophie became inseparable and always traveled together. God bless them both.

Likewise Capt. Shriver kept in touch with Stella, who remained at the Lodge throughout this initial rebuilding period. She was used to his six month-long deployments, so this separation was not so stressful for her that he couldn't keep her comforted again through the use of the shortwave radio contacts. And my suspicion was that by the end of another one or two months, he would be able to return to be with her. That was because one of the main objectives of the rebuilding was to unite family members wherever possible.   It was that unspoken goal which would serve as the backbone of this staggering recovery process.

And I suppose that brings me to the last of us Wagoners' contribution in this rebuilding effort; to Wally, Flo and myself. But before I begin, let me add that I am so relieved that during this time Wally did not have me perform any more of those vision-producing scratches. The collar became non-existent for me once again, and I was able to assist Flo and Wally without worry or anxiety. Despite everything, I was feeling ever-hopeful about our future. Even with all the destruction and loss of life, I felt a buoyancy and optimism about the days ahead. I guess it's just my nature to be this way.   I see the promise in everything!

TEN: THE DISSOLUTION

Now from a totally different perspective, I need to give you what Wally, Flo and I have been doing for these last three months, starting moments after Wally's soon-to-become tiresome routine of converting the three of us again and again into Canadian geese.

It had to be a hang-up of some sort with him. I would have preferred something trimmer; say a tern of some kind or possibly even a hummingbird. Did you know, while you and I are somewhat idling our time at this point, that there are some species of hummingbirds that fly from places like Georgia to southern Mexico, non-stop, across the Gulf of Mexico? (How else could they, considering there is nothing but water underneath them?) I guess they gorge themselves before departure and then hit the 'road', so to speak. But, I mean, how much can they eat anyway? Whatever you might think about hybrid or all-electric cars, that feat of theirs requires mucho miles per gallon. They have a fuel-efficient engine that engineers and environmental scientists should sincerely investigate for vehicle engines of the future. With my appetite, if I had the same ergonomic efficiency as they do... and, of course, wings... I could probably fly cross-country four or five times on one fill-up. In addition, if I was transformed into an oversized hummingbird, I wouldn't have all this itchy, bristly hair... and no blasted Wally-collar!

Speaking of which, the magic collar does not change sizes or shapes like I do during these transformation episodes. It just clangs around my long goose-appearing neck as I fly. It's so embarrassing when I once land and if someone sees me; it appears I tried to put my head into something I shouldn't have, and it got stuck. Maybe if it was engraved with some endearing phrase or football logo I might feel less self-conscious. But it just hangs there until I return to my usual, 'Greg-the-now-dog' self. Over time, I began to sigh heavily when Wally announced we had to resume our flying appearances again. I once asked him if he could just attach wings to my dog body, but he just walked off mumbling something about the inherent genetic deficiency of some dog's brains.

But I have departed from my somewhat bias version of what happened to the three of us in those months after we left the Lodge.

But never fear, there will be others who do a much more thorough job and do it from a much less emotional perspective. I tend to take things too personally, I suppose....

Anyway, our flight back-tracked somewhat over the areas we saw when we returned northward from our first survey of the terrible damage down to the tip of coastal, northern California. Now, instead of flying north through the Willamette Valley, we were flying south toward and into the interior of California. And once we departed the ruined, southern suburbs of southern Portland and reached the northern edges of the Willamette valley, it soon became clear to the three of us that this was to become one of the major new settlement areas for survivors.

The 2,500 individual communities were springing up across the length and breadth of this extended valley, as well as those valleys bordering or split by the Rogue River in southern Oregon and within the irrigated, high desert valleys of central Oregon. It appeared the Cascade Mountain range protected most of the dams in central Oregon; the ones which impound the necessary water for their irrigation. It was a godsend for the survivors throughout the Northwest. For even though the mountain roads and passes had been made impassable by the earthquakes and aftershocks, the Columbia River still offered enough of a 'highway' down and around the mountains to get foodstuffs to the western side of them... as long as the residents accepted that they had to ration any fuel for emergency use and for food transport only.

The valley terrain we passed over appeared relatively unscathed by the quakes. But of course the cities situated within them, e.g. Eugene, Salem and Medford had suffered terrible damage and were no longer recognizable. The variety of lush greens that stretched across these valleys seemed to signal that life was still possible, that food and shelter could still be grown and built. It gave the three of us hope as we flew over. But these places were not our destinations.

More ominous were the mountain roadways and highways that Interstate 5 interconnected with or coursed through. Once someone left the Cottage Grove area, the roads became impassable due to landslides and downed bridges. And this only became worse after you left Ashland, Oregon. Roads which sliced through and around steep hillsides and mountainsides were now completely blocked and even covered... sometimes for miles and miles with debris, rocks and soil. And long stretches of various rivers in these areas were artificially dammed as well. There was no infrastructure left for commerce. Passage through most of southern Oregon and northern California along the main artery of Interstate 5 was now a thing of the past. I could only hope that a roadway might be operational further to the east, allowing travel from south to north. None existed on the western side of the Cascade Mountains in and out of Oregon and California.

It was when we reached the San Joaquin Valley that the immensity of what had happened to most of California leaped up at you.

No sooner had we soared over what used to be Lake Shasta, than we saw a huge, scoured basin with only the meek remains of a meandering Sacramento River coursing out of a gaping hole in what used to be Shasta Dam. The force of the earthquake had ruptured the dam. And in doing so, this caused the lake's brimming contents to rush into the valley below, sweeping away all of Redding and Red Bluff. (see Appendix: **The Sacramento River**) And for hundreds of square miles before us, you could only see the remains and debris of these cities, local farms and industries. It all lay in immense piles of rubble for as far as we could see.

Not even Chico was completely spared the flood's onslaught. But at least a sizable portion of it appeared repairable. Both the university campus and downtown were heavily damaged, but at least they were not swept away. There still appeared to be enough infrastructure left to allow rebuilding to proceed. And there were scattered clumps of people and vehicles attempting to recover and begin rebuilding.

Not being able to hear Wally very well when we were in flight formation, he nodded his head downward and then dipped his wings and lead us down towards a solid-looking, older building in the middle of town. He later explained that he wanted us to land and then review what we were going to do next. Once we did land, he immediately transformed us back again to ease our being seen as conversing without appearing too conspicuous.

Obviously, to anyone passing by, it would have appeared odd seeing three geese suddenly become a very small boy and two rather disheveled, wind-blown dogs.

And sure enough, we just landed and there standing not ten feet from us were a gentleman fellow and possibly his daughter. We soon learned that her name was Lilyanne, and the man standing beside her was indeed her father. It was also later learned that our landing here was not a spur-of-the-moment decision by Wally. This building, the Bidwell Mansion, was to become the headquarters for the Northern California Resettlement governing body; and the two individuals standing so close to us were to be instrumental in both that effort and organization. Meeting and getting to know them was one of the few pleasant highlights of our next three months.

And it probably should be noted at this juncture that I am dictating some of this material to Lilyanne to write down. There were just too many scenes to describe, emotions to confess and rebuilding efforts to record for me to remember it all before I could contact Bernie again. I had to tell someone who could then pass it on to her for storage and eventual distribution. It was an arbitrary decision on my part, and any oversight of what happened to me before then or what I saw during and after the three months or so after July 29th are entirely my fault. I would hope to see this record one day and maybe add to it, if there were obvious gaps in my immediate memory that I later could amend. So, excuse this apology, but I felt you, the potential reader of these harrowing days, should know how and who helped create this record.

And I know I should mention this apparent impromptu meeting and what occurred during it, even though I had no idea of its significance at the time. Nor did Flo, because she saw the same gesture Wally made that I did. And we began to see the same greeting, as it occurred with Lilyanne and her father, happening with countless other kids and children her age or a little older or younger as we traveled throughout California. Little did we know it also happened when we were not around in Oregon and Washington as well.

What did we see? It always appeared that he unsheathed his wand and then gently touched each of these children on their foreheads. It was the oddest thing. He'd never done this before, nor had we ever seen Walt do it. And certainly he never did it to Flo or me!

All I got was this stupid collar, and I know Flo would have loved to have had maybe a loose harness of some kind around her shoulders and back: something to remind her and others that she is or could have been a magnificent sled dog...a leader of the finest team anywhere, with a truly stout and brave heart.

It is often the simplest of gestures that would give each of us such a sense of being appreciated and instill much needed self worth by those we are closest to and who we know cherish and love us as we knew Wally did. None of us, two or four legged, are so strong or faithful that we don't deserve that extra touch or gift... that one something that connects our lives with that someone who is our one-true mate forevermore. It's a gift that expresses more than love and fidelity; it confirms a lasting bond that will never be broken.

Both Flo and I looked at each other that day and sensed in the other that what was happening with Wally and this young girl had significance well beyond our comprehension. But we also oddly sensed that we would never truly know what it was. It was my first foreboding about our future. Both of us were becoming aware of an impenetrable shroud approaching us. I tried to dismiss it as stress-related fatigue and weariness from all we had witnessed and were doing. But it was becoming a nagging presence.

However, once he came back over to where we were waiting, he did notice our quizzical looks, and I'm sure he knew we saw his every move. But he said nothing that explained his action or motive. It wasn't until two months later when we were resting after this exhausting period of desperately trying to help the recovery effort in this now-forlorn State that he spontaneously, without any prompting from Flo or I, mentioned all the names of the children and kids that he had touched and spoken to, similar to the way he did that day in Chico. He just blurted out a litany of names, like it was something he was both relieved and proud to be able to list. It was the oddest thing. I recall them vividly. They were Aly, Lila, Spankie, Alexis, Jacob, Connor, Auggie, Nolan, Michelle, Patrick, Helen, Issac, Vincent, Sebastian, Melinda, Jason, Bianca, Brent, Zac, Elih, Lori, Olive, Natalie, Hope, Damien, Jude, Tyler, Serena, Angela, Stuart, Steven and Chris. Counting the first young girl he spoke with, he added that there were thirty-three in all.

And as he purposefully looked away after mentioning them, Flo and I looked at each other stunned. It was the exact number of new communities, like the ones Sophie was observing and reporting on to Frank and Capt. Shriver, which we had been overseeing and nurturing since their earliest stages of development. More specifically, this was the number of ALL the settlements left in the coastal portion of the western United States. There could be no more. This portion of the country could not support any more. The resources were too scarce, and the population had been either decimated or had to be evacuated elsewhere, as mentioned earlier.

This meant that given the strict guideline of only 2,500 residents per community that there were now only 82,500 individuals living in this entire, coastal, three State region. And when you consider the relatively small towns on the eastern side of the State, e.g. Susanville, Bishop and Barstow, most of which had experienced their own losses and migration, the grand total of people then trying to live in California was now only about 50,000. And there were somewhere around 38 million before July 29th!! It was just too staggering to dwell on for long.

But, for now, I need to get back to our assignment, as outlined by Capt. Shriver. And it started there in Chico. Despite the flood waters inundating the eastern half of the city from the Sacramento River and the loss of life associated with the earthquake itself, there were still about 15,000 survivors within about a ten mile radius of the city, which used to have a population of 87,000. Quite possibly, many were part of the refugee stream coming from all the area north of Fresno. Any survivors from Fresno south were to find shelter within the valley or join the migration through the Tehachapi Mountains, the only semi-passable route south or east. Nothing sustainable existed to the west, and the passage north was blocked by troops. All total, it was anticipated that five or six new, post-earthquake size communities could be erected and sustained in the foothills, near continuous flowing streams or riverbeds. Or in other words the tally of people left trying to rebuild in the southern half of the State was 12,500 to 15,000! Further south from what used to be Bakersfield had to be totally evacuated eastward into neighboring States and beyond. Southern California was declared uninhabitable.

While in Chico, Flo and I immediately began helping where and how we could while Wally reassumed being a feathered creature of various sorts. He took it upon himself to locate the seven areas most likely to provide a safe and sustainable environment for rebuilding. None of them, however, were to be within the Chico city limits. And it was at the first of those sites that he apparently had the young girl and her father immediately head toward after locating it.

It was very confusing to me what he was doing, but at least he hadn't extended that blasted staff of his and mumbled strange words, so I knew he wasn't creating chaos along the way. It all must have been purposeful. Flo and I were not privy to knowing what this secret business was all about. Secrets... that's so human...

Meanwhile Flo and I retained our natural state, which was comforting. Transforming back and forth from animal-to-bird has unusual consequences throughout your body... just you try it and see. Take having no ears for instance, where long, shaggy ones used to hang; or having a nice long tail, which now only sported feathers. There was nothing to wag or to have stand perfectly erect, signaling a sense of complete attention. And then there was the whole issue of teeth. I don't know how birds manage without them. Pecking is truly "for the birds". Give me something meaty and burley to dig my teeth into, and I feel like I'm alive. Nibbling at kernels of corn in some half frozen field or waddling into some smelly swamp for insects or minnows is pointless and demeaning. So both Flo and I were relieved to be our true selves for a while. We just let Wally dart about wearing the feathers.

Instead, we pretty much followed the instructions given to Jennifer and Rita. Flo was able to speak with a countless number of birds who were resting or nesting in the immediate area where we first landed in downtown Chico. From that point, the emergency response network began to form and extend throughout the habitable portion of northern California. For myself, I began enlisting all the four-legged critters of any size or shape to help guard, protect and defend what needed to be.

And again, because of all the destruction from the earthquake and resulting fires, it was determined that all settlements had to be established miles from Chico's previous city limits. No city services existed, and the clean up job was beyond what the survivors could manage and still be able to sustain themselves. Survival itself became the overriding goal for everyone. And helping in this process were the few uniformed security personnel remaining, along with Air Force personnel from the nearby, but now completely destroyed Beale Air Force Base and scattered members of the Reserve and National Guard. Along with these uniformed personnel, the process of deputizing civilians began in earnest. Wally was quite active in that process, as well as performing some 'slight-of-hand' with his collapsible staff and wand to secure desperately needed supplies.

I don't know how that little tyke kept it all together, but whenever we did have time to rejoin one another during that hectic two weeks, I began to notice the slightest bit of temper and disappointment creeping into his manner and voice. Who could blame him? I suppose even if you are a wizard, one's age has to be recognized as a limiting factor in some way, especially if you are only seven years old, which I have to proudly note, again, is the same age as myself. But despite everything that was happening to us, all I could do was worry about him.

Actually, both Flo and I worried. That Flo has such an uncanny ability to see what's truly inside someone. She knew long before I did the effect all this turmoil and resettlement was having on the lad. We worried together. Wally and Bernie were such precious gifts to this world; and you could begin to sense their glowing, inner lights were beginning to dim and flicker. Nature's lack of feeling and tendency for dispassionate destruction and death were taking its toll on all of us. And I am too dumb to know why or if there is any Force or Being that exists or counters it all. Surely, a little boy's magical devices alone are not anywhere near enough. The countless stars one sees at night indicate the Universe is too big and indifferent for even these two brave souls to protect, rebuild and heal what can be broken and lost so quickly and so impersonally.

Anyway, after two weeks in the Chico region, the process of selecting sites and shuffling survivors to them had well begun. Flo and I had roamed the nearby hills for recruits to help each settlement, and Wally was finally satisfied that the process had enough momentum to proceed without us.

So returning to the Bidwell Mansion grounds, he

met one last time with that same child and her father, like I eventually saw him do so many times with his other seemingly special children, and then the three of us were transformed back into geese and soared off to points south. Our next destination was the San Francisco area.

And it being over three weeks since we left the Lodge, as we approached the Bay Area we could still see a pall of smoke over the entire area. The closer we got, the horror of what had occurred that one day in July became almost too horrible for us to look down upon.

It was like some unseeing, mammoth hand, clutching onto an immense wire brush had scrubbed the landscape clean, aside from the still huge, smoldering piles of downtown buildings in what used to be Oakland, San Francisco and San Jose. As far as we could see, through the haze, everything was burned, broken or buried… if it wasn't just completely scoured clean, it was piled up against the surrounding hillsides.

All the bridges were down. All highways were impassable to vehicles, other than whatever detours the few remaining stragglers could manage on foot or riding bicycles. And there were still individuals winding their way out of these cities and surrounding communities into the interior. There was no sign of any relief organizations. The decision had been made to completely abandon the area. Who knew when there might ever be reoccupation again? Hundreds of thousands had lost their lives in the minutes during and after those unprecedented events. It was too much to look at. And yet Wally said we had to do a thorough survey and try to help anyone who needed it here, and then do the same further south in Los Angeles, San Diego and then on our return trip to the Sacramento area. It was like a death flight.

Compounding our anxiety and weariness of trying to be helpful in an environment that completely defied how that was supposed to be done, plus it was now fully evident that absolutely no federal help was coming, there was now an eerie feeling I had that we were somehow being followed. This latter feeling became more and more nerve-wracking once we arrived in the Bay Area. And for the longest time I said nothing. Finally, when the premonition became so strong, I hesitantly asked Flo if she, too, had felt any such surveillance. Most shockingly, she did.

We decided not to bother Wally with our worries. He had more than enough to occupy his thoughts; the most bothersome being where was the needed help from the federal government. There was none.

It was like my second vision predicted. And I knew then it foretold worse things to come. This series of events and the overwhelming loss of life and property had exposed the gap in our nation's drift into unacceptable and far-reaching, self-destructive behavior. More than the western States were now at risk... I sensed this for the first time that moment. If we couldn't help our own in times like this, we were prime for radical, even revolutionary changes in the near future. I was becoming more scared for our own immediate future and for the country's by the day. I just hoped keeping busy would chase these worries away.

So, swooping down we began a most heartfelt, but ineffective attempt at helping relieve some of the suffering for those trying to exit the region. And to do so, Wally began by using whatever wizard-given skills he could to relieve and sustain the struggling survivors as they marched through and around the rubble to safety and to a temporary shelter or evacuation route to another State to the east. Primarily, through the use of his trusty wand and staff, he created self-serve resting and sleeping stations every five miles; and these extended from San Francisco's southern city limit's the length of California to the Arizona border. These aid stations followed the highway system out of Oakland, San Jose and San Francisco out to Interstate 5 on the western side of the San Joaquin Valley and over to Highway 99 on the eastern side and up and over the Tehachapi Mountains to Mojave and over to the Arizona border where motorized transportation was readily available to evacuate anyone all points east into the mainland. These life-saving stations provided restroom facilities, cots, food and water.

And Flo and I spent those two weeks in a concerted effort to round up all the stray animals in the area and deputize them to be both alert to any health needs of the evacuees, but to also provide additional security at the aid stations. Each station was to have at least five dogs and various sized species of the cat family, and they were to insure no one took advantage of one another in these shelters. There's nothing like a mountain lion watching your every move to discourage you from pilfering or shaking down some weary traveler. Criminal acts or the urge to commit them were almost non-existent in these rest areas, but that's not to say there weren't problems along the way outside them.

Bad behavior, leading to actually harming others, was something that puzzled me under these awful circumstances. And it did not have to take the form of physical contact or purposeful intimidation. Simply ignoring the desperate needs of the citizens attempting to survive and negotiate their way out of their destroyed homes and cities easily qualifies someone as behaving badly. And those in seats of power and influence in the nations' governmental centers were displaying a grand disregard and apathy for us out here. Criminal acts don't have to be overt. They can be so subtle as to almost seem humanitarian... even to those complicit in this deceitfulness.

For every act of bravery and sacrifice we saw during these days and weeks following July 29th, we saw just as many examples of sorry behavior... if not more. And it worried us... especially Wally. This was not the way it was supposed to turn out. This is not what Walt, Willa and Po had sacrificed and worked so hard to have happen. This tragedy exposed the underbelly of the government and those who were in charge. Each of us in those days we worked in the Bay Area became more and more concerned about what we were seeing. And the sense of being watched or followed became even more intense during this time.

And it was not our having over-active imaginations. Flo and I were sure of that. But we hesitated to ask Wally whether he was also feeling it. He had too much on his mind for us to bother him with more problems. Instead, we proceeded to fly down to Los Angeles for our next two week layover.

On the way, we diverted somewhat and flew over Fresno, south of which there were to be established some of the new communities, although not as many as were to be built in the northern section of the valley. All the ones in the southern half had to be located close to some free-flowing stream or river for now. Drilling for water would possibly extend their number later, but there was no time, trained personnel or equipment for it to be done right away.

It was all a mournful sight, just the same. There was still a pall of smoke in the valleys from smoldering ruins. Frankly, I don't think there could have been a stronger series of earthquakes, without the earth opening up and letting lava spew up over the countryside. We saw very little human activity all the way down to the Los Angeles basin.

And once there, starting with our entering the Antelope Valley, there were no passable highways or any structures that looked intact. Sweeping into the San Fernando Valley, we only saw stragglers trying to make their way to embarkation points to be evacuated from what was left of this portion of the once, magnificent State of California. The normal haze of automobile and industrial pollution had been replaced with that of smoke from countless pyres... of homes, office buildings and industrial complexes. But most heart-breaking of all was to see the aftereffects of the tsunami on the region.

The mammoth waves showed no mercy. They swept over two miles into the basin at some points. And wherever the towering waves' fury ended, there were hundred-foot high mounds of destruction extending as far as the eye could see. It meandered southward into the horizon. And in front of these immense debris mounds, there was nothing until you saw the new shoreline, lying there as if in wait to pounce once more onto any who ventured into the scarred death zone. This area was completely barren of all life, intact buildings or foliage. It was as if some mighty hand had taken bleach, along with a giant shovel and broom and scraped and swept until there was nothing left. We all just gasped as we flew over this merciless killing zone.

Circling Los Angeles' huge city limits repeatedly until he was satisfied that it was senseless to attempt landing anywhere in the region, Wally finally indicated that we would try hop scotching over any likely refuge areas in the easternmost portion of its outlying suburbs. And it was there we began our, by now, customary assignments to help. But there were to be no new settlements established, as mentioned before. We just tried to make sure the remaining survivors were strong enough to make the trip east... out of the State. This once mighty and beautiful jewel of a city and region were now to be returned to a desert sanctuary.

The loss of life that occurred here made this hallowed ground. And the lack of federal response to this tragedy made it the crossroad for defining our future, national identity. You couldn't help but sense that what both happened and didn't happen here would soon shape more than just the lives of the evacuees. Even I knew this country was about to become radically changed forevermore.

From Los Angeles, with mounting weariness, we flew over to San Diego, where it was a replay of what we had seen in San Francisco and Los Angeles. There were no standing bridges, no downtown structures intact and no signs of anything living for at least a mile inland.

Any migration had been somewhat more organized here. I figured that was due, in part, to the presence of the Marine and Naval Bases in the area. Even though they each suffered terrible losses and destruction, the remaining personnel were able to mobilize and tend to any survivors before transporting them to various rendezvous points much further inland. By the time we arrived, we saw very few non-uniformed personnel in the shattered streets or countryside bordering this once, metropolitan area. But Wally still wanted to alight and have us comb the region, enlisting whoever and whatever we could to provide support and protection for those yet to be evacuated.

I didn't see him speak to any children, like he had in the San Francisco and outlying Los Angeles areas. The only remaining ones he spoke with, and always seemed to touch on their forehead with his wand, were at my hoped-to-be, last stop in Sacramento. And that was only a week away. We had been on this mission of Capt. Shriver's for almost three months, and each of us wanted to return back to the Lodge as soon as possible.

I, in particular, wanted to demonstrate to Goodie what a good provider I could be. My hopes for our future had only grown since we went on this mission. Absence, and becoming fonder, seems to always go hand-in-hand, as they say.

And through these past weeks, the impression of being watched became more fixed and unnerving. At one point, I even saw what looked all-the-world like Goodie at a distance staring at Flo and me. Certainly, whoever it was had that same intense, detached look I saw in the window at the Lodge that day of my second Wally-vision. Flo wasn't with me this time, so I never said anything to her about it. I figured it had to have been fatigue playing tricks on me.

Just the same, Flo later that same day remarked how uneasy she felt. Her instincts were telling her that we were in danger and that we needed to go back home. Something was very wrong. And, indeed, she felt someone or something was tracking us, waiting for an unguarded moment to pounce. She felt we were very vulnerable so far away from the other Wagoners. We both knew it was with them that our strength was greatest. Even with our being with Wally was not enough protection, she sensed. We needed to hurry along.

Her confiding this to me did nothing to relieve my

own misgivings. So immediately after that we approached Wally and said we wanted to leave and head back to the Sacramento area. Oddly, his look at our suggestion was equally alarming. It was one of fear. And on that small boy's face, it was more frightening than anything I had seen in this last year. I was now scared through and through.

Flo and I did not contribute much to the rebuilding effort in the Sacramento area. Again for the next two weeks, Wally did perform his now-customary introductions and wand touches to a few scattered children and then worked with the organizing teams for the new communities being started south of the city, adjacent to both year-round streams and in the shelter of wooded hillsides. These, and the others already started, totaled the thirty-three communities in the western United States which now had organizing committees and refugees streaming into each of them. A new Far West was emerging, and it was time for us to head home.

It was our next to the last day there that Wally had me relay all the material that I had not previously shared with Lilyanne in Chico to Bernie. To do so, I spoke to her on a local shortwave radio connection that Wally had found.

And Bernie, bless her heart, was fully capable of remembering every word. Oh! That I could have been a Herald...

It was after we awoke the next morning and became more and more alert, along with having something to eat, that Wally approached Flo and I and announced that he was extremely concerned about the disturbing activity here and elsewhere over these last three months. In the time we slept, which Wally never seemed to do, he used some of the special powers given to him by Walt that he had never used before to transport himself throughout the nation. It was something Walt had told him to only do when a situation appeared dire. And his travels over these three months proved his premonitions were well founded. Attitudes and behaviors throughout the nation were becoming more than just minor misbehaviors. People, in all levels of government and throughout the society, seemed bent on not behaving at all. As anxious as I have ever seen him, he requested that I perform the necessary maneuvers to experience the Third and Final Vision, the one involving the state of the nation.

His concern and revelation were in stunning contrast with the almost unreal dedication and tireless efforts demonstrated by the survivors we had been working with to unite and rebuild. However, as I studied him, following his making this request, I could tell there was something more personal bothering him. Being a dog and being so close to someone like my very special buddy, Wally, naturally meant that I could sense things that even his fellow humans couldn't. He was deeply afraid. And it was of something more immediate and local than whatever shenanigans the so-called leaders and wayward citizens to the east of us were dithering with. And I further sensed it was the same thing that had been bothering Flo and me for these last weeks. We were being watched very closely and skillfully. We were under threat, and Wally knew it.

Realizing this somehow made me calmer. I knew my magical friend could solve any problem and overcome any hostile intent. So, looking around to make sure no one would see my bazaar antic of lying on my back, while also attempting to scratch the collar, I then lay down, rolled over on it and scratched. Immediately thereafter, the vision process began; my very last one I assumed and desperately hoped.

It began with noise, which stunned me. There was a rumbling that grew louder and louder, like what you might expect from a landslide. Then I saw little rocks being shaken loose, followed by bigger and bigger ones, all assembling together to bounce and heave down a long and steep mountainside... with me in an enclosed valley below. The noise built and built. It became frighteningly loud and intense. I felt the need to scream and pull myself out of the vision, but I couldn't. It was now like a nightmare I couldn't awaken from. I was trapped and confined. The roaring mass was heading straight for me... and oddly, beside me were standing Flo and Wally, each paralyzed as well. But then it all stopped and there was deafening silence.

And before me, in the distance, stood Walt and Willa, just as sure as if I was sitting at their feet at Willa's farmhouse. They both motioned for me to come closer. As I did, they both sat down in a couple of ornate, oversized armchairs. Surrounding them and me were long, flowing tapestries, woven with unmatched skill, incorporating every imaginable color and depicting various individuals and activities. There must have been at least one hundred of them, representing the greatest events or moments in this tattered and overly exhausted world.

They each continued to beacon me forward, despite my reluctance and hesitation to be a part of this vision-generating process, along with the now bazaar illusion of seeing my dear companions again. I began to slow my pace and became frightened. It was all too real. Then Walt spoke.

"It's alright, my trusty friend. Come forward and

sit with us... dearest Greg. You are safe here. We need to speak with you one last time while you and the Wagoners are still intact. The future for all of you is about to rapidly change, far beyond what you could have anticipated happening. Because of these upcoming changes, Willa and I need you to perform one last act before they do. And don't worry; you will remember all that I tell you and all that you will see and experience during this vision. I will insure that you do. Your message must be passed along to Bernie and Wally as soon as we are finished here.

"I need to speak to you about what is plaguing this world now that the Emissaries have been banished. It is the one last and, most likely, the final, true threat to all life on this world. It is bad behavior, a seemingly bland problem one might argue. But I am not talking about something like you barking uncontrollable in the back of Frank's pickup truck bed, nor of some silly misbehaving between you and Wally, teaming up against Jennifer or Rita. I am speaking of truly bad, rampant behaviors that are weakening the sustaining fabric of your nation and this world.

"First off, probably a definition of what I am referring to is in order. Even you must have wondered from time to time what comprised someone or something displaying 'bad behavior'. And to answer this, it probably is in the same category as when someone once sagely described what 'pornography' was: 'You know it when you see it'. As a rule, everyone knows what it is, but it is too often impossible for them or possibly even you personally, to admit to acting in such a manner. It seems to be something that is always associated with someone else... not you. But each of us, including me, knows it when it happens... by others anyway.

"That said, what are the causes leading up to this

most insidious and now pervasive type of behavior? From all I've seen in my centuries of travels through and around your world, I'd reduce it to three main culprits. And they are: an individual's evolving, or in some cases his or her innate character; the organization or body he or she is living or working in or around; and finally there is the particular time or situation he or she finds themselves in at the time there is a lapse, an opportunity or a goading into this potentially destructive pattern of behavior.

"Sadly, it appears nearly anyone at one time or another can drift into or elect to act badly, even if they are of sound character and moral rectitude. It's no secret; human beings have their weaknesses, prejudices and desires... all of which can lead them into the steadily growing darkness of worsening behavior. And for some, this process regresses even further into the realm of becoming evil behavior. Simple mischievous or casual bad behaviors can widen into harming, even destroying others' lives. And it is this process that has led Willa and me to return in a vision to speak with you.

"The evil beings we fought in Oregon and those despotic regions you dismantled across the world throughout your oceanic travels are gone. We fear that now an almost, even more destructive force is spreading across this land and others. And I worry that there will be even fewer of you left to try and combat it. Time is running out for you, my loyal and resolute Wagoners. But you must get this message out to Wally and Bernie, despite the dangers I see ahead for all of you. This land is in crisis.

"Why the urgency, you must be wondering?

"It is because the risks, consequences and aftereffects of bad behavior are self-multiplying. Each of the following ones is so dangerous both for the errant individual, as well as for those beyond. They become a distorted evolution of normal behavior, creating a kind of inattention to the facts and the truth... as ethereal as it is at times to find or know what they or it is.

"When this type of behavior begins, almost immediately thereafter a fog of biases arises, clouding any judgment and perception of what really is and what it should be. These biases become 'anchored' or they rely entirely or far too much on too little information for mature and forthright decisions. They 'focus' or give too much weight to a single issue or feeling, which leads to gross and tragic errors for the outcomes that follow. They become 'wishful thinking', allowing unfounded beliefs or an insatiable imagination to ignore sound reasoning or reasonable evidence to the contrary. They led to 'irrational escalation', justifying and basing decisions on a cumulative history of personal investments and denying new evidence that the current decision-making process is wrong. And finally, they cause 'normalcy' bias or a failure to plan or know how to respond to a disaster, such as yours, which they consider is unlikely to happen or to be of much consequence. These last two biases characterize the behavior pattern leading to the failure at the federal level that has so astonished all of you after these disastrous events on July 29th.

"Such behaviors create an impotence of action and decision-making, such as is being witnessed on a nationwide scale with the minimal to no federal response to these earthquakes and floods. It fosters division... throughout the nation, within what used to be a functioning Congress and amongst the general population, including you and all the others who can now speak. It leads to mounting instabilities... too many people who are too unruly, too demanding, too lazy, too greedy, too arrogant, too rich, too poor, too fat, too dumb, too amoral, too entitled, too obsessed, too secular and in some cases too, so-called religious. Overall, there are now just too many 'too's'. In particular, it fosters a self-destructive willfulness to demand total and complete freedom… to do, to have, to be anything, even at the expense of others and of the common good.

"And finally and most sadly, there is now a condition which exists within this nation that limits any magical intervention. The amount of bias, babble, bluster and false beliefs has far outpaced Wally's abilities or power to change. The era of magic is over. Now only hard work, dedication to duty and almost daily sacrifice will alter the destructive spiral I see coming. There is a polarization on the horizon that will split this country apart, and as a final portion of this, your last vision, I will provide you with an image of what is ahead for this land, unless these cumulative bad behaviors cease… from the top echelon of government to its most humble of citizens. (see Appendix: **The Disunited States of America**).

"This now united land will become divided into seven, distinct sovereign States. And the reasons for this are varied and involve longstanding issues that couldn't or wouldn't be resolved. Old wounds festered; new ones arose. Out west, it will be primarily due to lack of representation, given the densest population centers were nestled along its coastline. The middle of the country has been more level-headed than most of the rest of the country and will become tired of being governed from either the west or east coast power and population centers. The southern tier divisions will be mostly along old, historical borders, whether arising from prior nationhood status or from civil strife. And the last division will be formed in an attempt to recapture the flavor of the original model for the country at its founding.

"The divisions between these now, almost inevitable breakups will create the sovereign States of Pacifica, Cascadia, Missoura, Texahoma, Lincoln, Appalachia and Katadan. Pacifica and Cascadia will be divided by the crest of the Cascade and Sierra Mountains as they sweep down onto the crest of the Joshua Tree Monument and over to the Colorado River. Cascadia will extend eastward to the crest of the Rocky Mountains down to the upper New Mexico border. Missoura will extend eastward to the Mississippi River and down to the same border defining the southern end of Cascadia. Texahoma will incorporate Oklahoma, New Mexico and Texas, with its easternmost border coursing along the western Louisiana border. Lincoln will be framed by the Mississippi and Ohio Rivers on their western, eastern and southern borders. Appalachia will be outlined by the Ohio River and include the State of Virginia along its northern border. Katadan will include Washington D.C. on its southern flank and sweep up to Buffalo on its northwest border.

"Each sovereign State will have access to the ocean or gulf, either directly or indirectly through a navigable river. And each will have its own self-governing body, border crossing checkpoints, requirements for citizenship, which will include a designated language by which all official business is conducted. Treaties and agreements can be struck with each other and with other nations for trade, commerce and immigration.

"In common with each of them will be a union of military forces and coast guard protection. There will be a central bank and a common currency, as is used by the European Union. Each will share in infrastructure upkeep and upgrades; these will serve the common good for commerce, trade and protection. And there will be a federal governing body, but it will have very limited powers and taxing ability. The total collapse of civil and useful federal legislating will ultimately be one of the critical developments leading to this disunion.

"There will be only a figurehead leader of the federation. Each sovereign state will have its own elected leadership, which will have limited terms of office. Each entity will have its own legislature and court, but a federal court will also remain in place. However, its rulings can be overturned by the ones in each sovereign State, should the voters indicate through their elections that it is necessary. All decisions will become local in nature. The power is returned to the people and these nationwide divisions were the only way that it was deemed possible to have this happen.

"However...remember... this is only a vision of what can happen, not something of absolute certainty. With you passing along the contents of this vision to Wally and Bernie, there is always the possibility that civil strife and permanent separation will be avoided. But there must be significant changes in the status quo at all levels of governing for this country for it to remain united. Otherwise, it will surely become the Disunited States of America.

"And finally, let us both extend to you our most deeply felt admiration and appreciation for what you, Flo, Rita, Jennifer, Sophie and Frank have done over this last year. Please express to all of them how grateful and proud we are to have been associated with each you. You are, to an individual, so brave and noble. And when your time comes to join me, we will welcome you warmly and lovingly for the eternity you each so richly deserve. Farewell for now, my dear Greg. Stay ever-strong and alert. Your forebodings are not unfounded."

.

ELEVEN: THE DECEPTION

Shaken to the end of my stubby tail following this stunning vision, I quickly flipped over and immediately rose up on my sturdy, four legs. I felt that was absolutely the last one of these vision-things I was going to do for Wally, Walt, Bernie or ANYONE. They left me too scared and bewildered. What in the heck was I supposed to do about all that I just saw and heard? And what sense could I make of who appeared and what was said in them? Being a shaggy dog doesn't give you all the talents and privileges that others have.

Immediately, I felt the desperate need to get Wally fully informed about what occurred and to contact Bernie and get this vision fully relayed before I begin to forget that it ever happened.

It took me the rest of the day to do just that. But it sure didn't make Wally feel any better... nor did it Flo, after she listened in to our conversation. So, once I finished my lengthy report to Bernie, a unanimous decision was made by the three of us to have Wally convert us once more and then lead us directly back to the Lodge. There was to be no stopping over to see Sophie, who fortunately had elected to return to the Lodge along with Bernie after my most recent report. When Wally told me that the two of them would be there by the time we got back, Flo and I both were so relieved. We needed the presence and comfort of those two. We were totally exhausted and depleted of energy and will.

And within the next twelve hours we were circling over the lake adjacent to the Lodge. Never in my life had anything looked so comforting. It was an incomplete homecoming; it being minus Jennifer, Rita and Frank. But it was so reassuring just the same. Everyone, including Sophie and Bernie, looked exhausted and drawn. Our telling them about the strange premonitions we each had throughout our stay in California appeared to confirm some of the misgivings the two of them had been having as well. Coming back together like this helped ease somewhat that tension. A certain relief and a glimmer of calm slowly began to comfort us.

And most exciting of all for me was when Happy and Goodie showed up the next day. Happy, of course, was his usual nosey self, wanting to be everywhere we were. Goodie, on the other hand, did appear somewhat withdrawn. She entered into conversations when all of us were together, but she didn't seem keen on being alone with me, like she was when we first met. I excused this as her probably being shy in an over-exuberant crowd.

But a few times I did notice a creeping sense of threat, even here at the Lodge. And mystifyingly, it almost always was accompanied with the entrance of Goodie into the room or when we were gathered outdoors. Though it was the middle of November, it was nice to still be able to spend a little time outside on the spacious lawn behind the

Lodge with everyone. Somedays, surprisingly for being late Autumn, it was almost idyllic. To have constantly been surrounded by such loss for all these last months had weathered each of us. Our guards were down. Our alertness was dulled.

But I went ahead anyway and confided these troubling thoughts and any inconsequential happenings to Bernie one morning, as I usually tried to do when we were together. It made it so much easier to recall anything and everything at the moment for her record keeping. Waiting like I did to report most everything we did and saw in California taxed me to the core. I wasn't EVER going to do that again.

I felt myself slipping deeper and deeper into a state of everlasting dogness. It was with such glee that I could be with Wally, Bernie and Flo these past few days. And to have Goodie in the neighborhood made it even more enchanting. Life, for me, was now good and only getting better.

And I finished my few final comments by asking Bernie if she wanted to go on a little hike with Wally, Flo and I tomorrow. Disappointedly, she said she couldn't due to having to contact Frank and Capt. Shriver about some suggestions she had for them and possibly her needing to return to the Lewis-McCord headquarters.

I was disappointed but said we'll all do it the next time, and she wholeheartedly agreed. Eagerly, I then joined my buddies and we went to bed early, after telling everyone our plans.................................... .

TWELVE: THE DISAPPEARANCE

.... I didn't have to go to Tacoma after all. But I was very busy all day getting messages back and forth to there and arranging meetings for when I would have to return. It wasn't until about 7 p.m. that evening that I asked where Wally, Flo and Greg were. No one knew. They had left at sunrise and had not been seen by anyone since.

At first I wasn't too alarmed. Wally would be able to wiggle out of any situation or magically transport them back here if they were lost.

But then Sophie came rushing into the main lounge area where I was sitting and cried out, "Oh, Bernie, I found Wally's staff and wand! He didn't take them with him today! Why would he have forgotten them?!! That's not at all like him. Do you think they could be in trouble?"

"Probably not," I replied, somewhat nonchalantly. "They were all three so excited about hiking further in towards the still-remaining, Olympic snow fields, he probably just forgot them. They'll no doubt stagger in sometime later this evening, famished and wanting to eat. Go ahead and go to bed if you like. I'm sure they're ok. If you see Happy or Goodie, ask them if they have any idea what might be the holdup."

"I already did. Happy had no idea. But I can't find Goodie anywhere. I've called and called; besides looking everywhere she usually is or might be. No one else can find her either."

"That's strange," I could only say. "Well, anyway, we'll give the three explorers more time before I will start to worry."

"You can count me as someone who is already there," Sophie answered, which seemed to me that she was being uncharacteristically anxious, almost to the point of being alarmed. Reluctantly, she soon left and made her way back to our common bedroom.

A little puzzled, I decided to sleep in the lounge that night, figuring I'd be the first one they would excitedly wake up to tell about their day's adventures. Soon enough, I was sound asleep from exhaustion. Their delay back did not concern me enough to prevent me from sleeping soundly until morning.

It was at daybreak that Sophie shook me awake exclaiming, "Wake up, Bernie!! They're not back!! I've asked everyone who is up and looked anywhere that they might have been sleeping. There is no sign of them!! Something is dreadfully wrong!! I feel it. We must launch a search for them right away!!"

Not being the morning person that Sophie and most of the Wagoners were, I had to take a moment or two to realize what she was so excited about. Once I did, it occurred to me that maybe they decided to spend the night due to their being so far inland, having reached their goal of the snowfields or even having reached the peak of Mt. Olympus. But even as I imagined that to be the case, I still felt the beginning pangs of deep concern.

Deviation from an outline of instructions or plans was not the customary way Wally approached the day... nor of Greg. Greg liked everything to fall neatly in line, as has been previously discussed. He might be a scatterbrain in many respects, but some order and defining timelines were essential for him to be fully engaged in a project or the day. Having these fundamental principles in place, then he could launch himself, headlong and pell-mell into a day. And I'm sure spending the night in a cold and damp overhang somewhere on a windy mountainside would not be in those prior plans of his.

Flo was even more so a stickler for detail and for following a given set of rules and agreements. Without a doubt, she is the more disciplined and organized of the three. If they had meant to spend the night, she would have let someone know that.

And as for Wally, well... given all he had been through these past months, maybe just this time he'd be along for the ride. His having to be preoccupied with so much tragedy these many months since our family's death in Atlantic City and with the awesome responsibilities since Walt's death probably gave him the perfect opportunity to jump at the chance to go hiking and camping with his best friends. No doubt that was the reason he left his wizard-craft implements behind.

But, still, I felt pangs of worry creeping into my consciousness. None of this made much sense to me. I needed to begin organizing a search party and call Frank and Capt. Shriver to let them know. They'd tell me how to proceed, if I was missing something in all this.

And by mid-morning, with still no word from or sign of the hikers, the first search party was launched.

Happy was to go along with them, following their scent as best the heavy morning dew and any overnight snow in the area would allow. Both Frank and Phil decided their earlier delay in not returning to the Lodge was no longer important enough for both of them not to return right away. Like Sophie, they sensed something was not right. And by noon, they had both arrived back here at the Lodge and began organizing another search party. They even set up a kind of command center to coordinate the search. It was about then that I became scared. Something was very wrong. The feelings of threat and of being observed, which each of them had mentioned to me, were now becoming a reality. Reaching down into my Herald-like attributes, setting aside for a moment my older-sister-to-a-little-brother assumptions, I sensed not just threat but bodily harm was at hand.

And where was Goodie in all this? My instincts began to focus on her as well. Why did she show up so conveniently those months ago, so prim and coiffed? And why had she so mysteriously disappeared as this drama was playing out?

But Frank told me to stay put. I was not to go on any of the search parties. They needed me here to stay by the shortwave radio and intercept any messages about rescue or discovery or even, God-forbid, any ransom demands. Kidnapping was one of the scenarios then being considered… along with their being just plain lost or one of them being injured and their not being able to travel as quickly as they had going into the wilderness.

All I could do was wait for some word. And the longer I waited the less hopeful I became that a rescue was likely. The deepest dread I had ever experienced began to seep its way into the depths of me. I began to pace. Hours passed and there still was no word. Until finally there was a crackling of the Lodge's shortwave, located a few paces from where I repeatedly turned at the far end of my back and forth pacing.

"Hello, Bernie! Are you there? This is Frank. Please pick up, if you hear me."

"I hear you, Frank," I replied. "Have you found them? Are they ok?"

"No, we haven't, Bernie," came his response, but in a grave tone. "But I'm afraid to say we have found confirming evidence of their presence here at one time. And it is not promising."

"What do you mean?" I almost cried out.

"There are definite signs that a mighty struggle has occurred," he added. "From what we can determine, Flo and Greg must have fought ferociously to save Wally. There are chunks of earth and broken branches scattered over a wide area, with clumps of their hair, bits of what appear to be teeth and blood stains everywhere."

"Are there any signs of Wally or either of the dogs?" I cried.

"We don't know what Wally was wearing, but there are pieces of cloth strewn about, and most disturbing of all, there is that collar that Greg was wearing. It has been torn into multiple pieces... almost as if someone knew its ability and wanted to prevent it from providing any further information about the future. But, sadly, there is no actual sign of any of them. All you can see is that a mighty struggle took place before our beloved companions were taken away... in whatever condition they were finally left in. You can almost hear and feel the ferocity of the fight by what you witness in this clearing. It's obvious our dear Wagoners were each giving their lives for the other."

151

"What do we do now?" I was barely able to ask.

"We are sending one group ahead to see if by chance there is any sign of them further on ahead. The rest of us are returning to the Lodge to launch a wider search for any type of aircraft or off-road vehicle that might have transported them away from here. It appears this fight happened sometime yesterday. I fear whoever took them has had plenty of time to get them far away from here."

"Where exactly are you?" I then managed to ask.

"We are at the tree line, just before the alpine meadows start. They must have been ambushed. Whoever did this, knew exactly their route and about the time they would emerge from the dense forest. And then the clearing provided them a quick exit from the area. And unfortunately, the weather was clear, allowing them a quick and easy departure."

"Please try to find them. Is there anything I can do at this end?"

"I'm afraid not. We've already sent word out to the folks at Lewis-McCord for some surveillance aircraft to be sent over and to alert everyone to be aware of any unusual activity or vehicles in their area."

"Ok, I'll wait for your return. I'm just devastated by this news, Frank."

"I know, Bernie. I know. But we must not give up hope for their rescue."

"Please hurry back," was all I could add. And then I hung up the receiver, knowing that it would probably take hours before they could get back to the Lodge.

But it wasn't more than thirty minutes after Frank's report that someone came running into the lounge area shouting that a seaplane of some sort was circling the lake behind the Lodge. It appeared that it was about to land on the water.

Everyone ran out to see, with me leading the pack. And sure enough a pontoon plane was skidding across the water, making its way toward the Lodge. But just as quickly, it suddenly turned 180 degrees, and it taxied to a stop. With its tail facing us we saw a rubber dingy being shoved out one of its doorways onto the water and someone getting in it. It had a motor of some kind attached to the rear of the inflatable boat and soon it was roaring in a circle and heading towards us.

Once it came close to the shoreline, its engine was cut off, allowing it to coast close enough to see the driver motion for someone to come forward. Sophie had already reached the water's edge and quickly waded far enough out to grab onto whatever was being transferred to her. And then just as quickly, the boat's engine was started up again and it skimmed the water back to the seaplane. Then, without loading the boat back into the doorway, once the boat's passenger got into the plane it began to taxi off toward the middle of the lake. Once it got out quit a piece, it turned again and faced the Lodge. At that point the engine was revved up and it began to speed towards us. And just as it was about to reach the shoreline it rose off the water and swooped over us.

Without knowing what the note or package said, I knew it had to have something to do with Wally, Flo and Greg's disappearance. In the noise that followed the plane's ascent and passing over us, Sophie motioned frantically for me to come forward to her.

By the time I reached her, she had climbed a few yards from the water's edge and was screaming something to me that I could not understand. Finally, as the plane flew well beyond the Lodge, I heard her shouting, "I saw

Goodie. She was sitting in one of the front seats of that plane. I'm sure it was her."

And then Sophie tore open the envelope that she had been handed. Reading it quickly, she slumped to the ground, as she handed it to me. Nervously, I took it and began to read:

'Let this be a warning to you!
Stop your meddling in national
affairs! This will be your only
warning. What has happened to
your associates, will surely happen
to each of you, if you should
persist in trying to radically change
the status quo of this nation.
Again this is to be your only warning.
Your three instigators are now
dead. The same fate will be yours,
if you persist further. No
more visions; no more ideas of
radical change or you
will face the same fate as theirs.
Signed,
The Guardians of Peace
and National Security'

THE FOURTH VISION

THIRTEEN: THE RESPONSE AND THE DETERMINATION

The shock and numbing horror of what we found and were later told kept all of us in an almost robotic state for the next five days. The search continued in the woods and alpine meadows for any sign of our loved ones. The investigation into who might have done this and what proof there was that what they claim happened... really did... also continued non-stop, as did the questioning of everyone over and over at the Lodge and in the nearby settlements for any clues.

Happy was interrogated endlessly about his role and his relationship to Goodie. And, as it turned out, he was not complicit in any way. Duped... for certain. Made a fool of... quite likely. But he was not a co-conspirator. And I do believe, despite his often thinly veiled jealousy of Flo and Greg, he felt sorry for this as yet, unconfirmed tragedy.

Goodie, on the other hand, without her presence ever after and the multiple sightings of her in the strangest places and times, including the possibility of her being in the cockpit of the seaplane's appearance five days ago, was considered the prime suspect for being the "inside" agent in this kidnapping and possible murderous act. And not forgetting as well, the note and its ongoing threat of more harm to come, if we proceed with our work and trying to uncover who did this.

It was only because of the anger that welled up inside me that I was able to function at all. Inside, I was full of grief and guilt. It should have been me they took. I was the one who daily functions as the nexus for funneling all information coming from sources throughout the westernmost States and then organizes and disseminates to whoever would be best to act on any updates. Wally, Flo and Greg were just facilitating scouts and do-gooders. They were at the periphery of whatever was happening in the rebuilding and reshaping process. It is I who they should have been targeting; not my brother and our two rescuers in Atlantic City.

Sophie and Frank, bless their hearts, had become almost immobile after the news. Their age and love of those three left them completely vulnerable and unable to stop mourning enough to help in the investigation. In all likelihood, I could sense that this action against us Wagoners may signal their gradual but steady retreat back to the sheltering love of their family members and well-deserved retirement. There is no way to measure the positive impact and vital roles they played in these past months, as we crossed the country, traveled across the oceans and then began the recovery process here in this ravaged region. I envied them their family ties. Mine were all severed now. With the growing likelihood of the loss of my little brother, I now had none. I was alone... without any relatives or immediate family.

Rita and Jennifer did arrive back here the day after the search party's discovery and the seaplane's appearance. And they have been a source of some comfort to me and are helping with the ongoing investigation. Rita has flown countless times over the region searching for any clues or suspects. And Jennifer has combed the surrounding woods for evidence. But neither has been able to provide much relief from my grief. It is just not in their nature to nurture or to provide comfort to someone in my present state. I understand this about them. And I still hope they will be at my side in the grueling weeks and months to come. I will need their eyes and ears close at hand.

Phil Shriver and Stella have worked tirelessly to collect the facts and coordinate the search parties, both military and civilian. Despite our clumsy appearance that evening aside the Polar Wind, before our around-the-world cruise, Capt. Shriver has become a vital ally and pivotal figure in the region-wide, rapid rebuilding response. And Stella has been everywhere at once trying to help in our local recovery. Everyone loves her.

That leaves me, and what I am supposed to do in light of the unconfirmed events that we have experienced and the threats that we have subsequently received. Right now, as I write this, I feel the most important task is to pursue the investigation and get as much confirmation of our loved ones' status and of those who are the culprits. I'll begin to formulate the proper response later. And rest assured there will be one. I am more determined than ever to overturn the system that has produced such arrogance and entitlement to power and wealth.

****

Then, soon after I wrote these thoughts, we had another shock… it was a most devastating one. It came by way of a courier, someone who was obviously oblivious as to what he was carrying or why. It was addressed to me. And inside the package was a video tape, which then took us some time to find a player that would allow us to see what was on it.

Once we did, its contents were indescribable. It showed in gruesome detail the final moments of the lives of my three, closest loved ones. Each of them appeared totally spent in their final moments. It was obviously clear that they had fought valiantly to protect each other. It was the worse thing I have ever seen or imagined I ever would. And off to the sidelines were the gloating faces of Goodie and her accomplices. It was as if they were goading us, knowing that we were powerless to find or prosecute them. It was as if they smugly knew they had each of us now in their sights as well.

Seeing the savagery of what they did, I arranged a meeting with Frank and Phil and suggested that each of us needed to be placed into some kind of protective custody. They agreed, saying that Joint Base Lewis-McCord would provide the most secure location for the time being. Even Sophie and Frank's families needed to be transported there, along with Rita and Jennifer. All of us were now considered targets. And it was there, over the next few weeks that I began the process of self-examination, meditation and strategizing to help this precious land regain its optimism and hope for the future. To do so would entail a total revamping of all aspects of governing and daily functioning. And it would upend the smug world of the power elite and their lackeys.

Unlike Greg's remarkable visions, which were delivered while he was in a state of semi-consciousness, mine were conscious, occurring to me while I was fully alert. And they occurred over a period of weeks; not in minutes as they were with poor Greg. I essentially sequestered myself all this time, only coming out of my self-imposed isolation to eat and visit briefly with whoever was not in route somewhere on business. However, after the deaths of our companions, there was little travel without adequate security personnel accompanying any of us. But I had no desire to travel or leave our compound. I had to finish what Wally, Flo and Greg had begun.

Their sacrifice, prompted by Greg's visions, had to be honored in some way by my suggesting a meaningful roadmap for rebuilding and retaining the unity and innate goodness historically demonstrated over and over by the citizens of this land. The deterioration of behavior at all levels of our society had to be addressed to foster and preserve its unique role in this world. And I sensed the children who Wally had chosen to be a part of the new communities had a vital role to play as well in this rebuilding process.

Finally, after two months of agonizing trial and error with what measures I felt were needed, I was able to present Frank and Phil my reconstruction plan; the outlined of which is below. The timelines for its implementation will follow afterward.

There are five distinct activities or bodies that I have decided were in need of behavioral reform. They are voting, governing at the federal level, the economy, Congress and each individual citizen. And in case something should happen to me, as was the case with my dearest brother and friends, I need to write down what I sense needs to be done. Copies of this will be given to the various appropriate individuals once it is finished.

To begin with, I should probably start with Congress, which in a way should be the easiest place to begin enacting the necessary changes. It is in this branch of government that one sees the most egregious faults and lapses. There is a bloated sense of entitlement and self-righteousness that cries out; reform of this institution is long overdue. It has become ingrown and inept. And it is impossible to accept its present membership and dysfunctional attempts to govern any longer... as it is currently so smugly self-managed. Everything from term limits, tenure, benefits, pay raises and how it behaves when doing the People's Business has to be changed. (see Appendix: **Congressional Reform Act of 2012**) The timelines for these changes will be outlined later, as previously mentioned.

Serving in Congress is an honor. It, in itself, cannot become a career. While The Founding Fathers did foresee that some outstanding individuals might need to become longstanding members, this well-meaning expectation has morphed into a professional vocation of most members, with their constituents captivated by the "earmarks" that come to their respective districts. Almost its entire membership has become mired in with an elite, privileged class which only seems to patronize their subjects. If someone stays in office long enough the rewards, kickbacks and perks become hypnotizing and corrupting. All-too-often, statesmanship is rarely the outcome for long term residence in Congress.

And as if this institution's lost moorings is not enough, over the last several decades it has lost the ability to govern. It has become a centerpiece for bad behavior at the highest level and now presently is leading the way as the most serious threat to our Republic's continued existence. Our Constitution outlines in sufficient detail what Congress is commanded to do. It is the vital link of governance that balances the power of the Executive and Judicial Branches. But it probably would not be too off the mark to suggest that a Second Constitutional Convention is probably going to be necessary to reinforce and update the expectations of that First Constitutional Convention. (see Appendix: **The Constitution of the United States of America** (abridged))

The list of omissions, distortions and acquiescence's by Congress is breath-taking. More and more, Congress is becoming the hand-maiden for the Executive Branch; that is, when it is not dead-locked in a polarized and uncompromising standoff by the two parties. The middle ground of governance has become a barren wasteland, where no one wants to be seen as unfaithful to their particular party. It cannot be overstated; there is a constitutional crisis within this Body, particularly as it relates to the Executive Branch of government. Our survival as a Republic is now at stake. This terrible series of recent, West Coast calamities has overexposed the ineptness of our federal government. Change is no longer an option; it is now a vital part of the rebuilding for us here in the West and for this nation.

Next, we come to the third activity that needs reforming in this frightfully vulnerable land: voting. This most sacred obligation and most treasured duty in any democracy has become diluted by gerrymandering, bribing, intimidation, and most of all by a poorly educated and inadequately prepared public. Just as governing has become weakened, so voting has become dangerously contaminated by abuses and laziness. It, above all else that this nation brought forth in its fight for freedom and equality, is the beacon to the rest of the world.

Voting by this nation's citizenry is the most precious gift we have given civilization. But it has become diluted and manipulated in recent years. Certainly, the Emancipation Proclamation, the long overdue inclusion of women's right to vote, the civil rights era's enfranchising those long-denied this birthright and the welcoming of legal immigrants to this land are all hallmarks of a nation coming to grips with its sins and errors and opening its arms to others. But new dangers are rising with the carelessness now seen in the voting process. Changes have to be made in this most important act of our democracy. (see **Appendix: Voting Reform Act of 2012**).

The next activity, if you will, that needs addressing in this, our desperately final attempt to steady our Ship of State and keep it from sailing headlong into swallow shoals and become forever disunited, is the need to modify and change the financial wilderness we are lost within. Personal and public debt; an overall sense of entitlement; over-inflated prices of goods and services; the loss of our manufacturing base, which has plunged us into being an import-dependent puppet of the world; a laziness of spirit, which has led to an overblown sense of self-worth and finally our being mesmerized by thinking manipulation of electronic gadgetry signals intelligence and creativity have all replaced study, hard work and sacrifice. It is here, especially, that all of us must combat this collective decline in normal behavior. And it is here that our land is probably at its most vulnerable. And to remedy this sorry regression, a galactic shift in our daily lives will be necessary. (see Appendix: **Financial Reform Act of 2012**).

Now I need to outline the timelines for these reforms to take place. And while timeliness is of the essence in both our rebuilding and preventing the Union dissolving into separate, sovereign States, there will still have to be a staggered timeframe for fully instituting these changes. There is already enough chaos and discontent raging throughout growing pockets in this land, without thrusting all these changes at everyone at once.

During the first year, aside from the individual behavioral changes necessary in each of us, which have to begin immediately, Congressional reforms should be completed. That is to be theirs and the country's first order of business. In addition, by the end of this first year, the first Consumer Assessment Index, or CAI, recommendation for the devaluation of all goods, services, wages and housing should be completed. It will be instituted overnight; just like the changing of our clocks is done twice a year for Daylight Savings. It will be immediate and universal.

The second year will involve using the first voting reforms in our election process. By this time, all the necessary changes will have been instituted in counties across the country and people will have had time to learn enough English to read or understand what is being read to them to pass the mandatory tests.

At the end of the third year the full range of financial reforms should be in place. Debt reduction, balanced budgets, taxation models, cooperatives, banking and financial institutions standards and a vastly increasing level of exports will have been achieved.

And by the end of the fourth year there will be full implementation of the new taxation laws; there will no longer be any need for income tax collection. High savings and investment levels for rebuilding the infrastructure and manufacturing base of the country; a return to hard work at a wage that allows a family to easily afford housing; straightforward laws and rules at all levels of government and pride and confidence once again in the three major branches of our government should then be well in place.

And now, we have come to the last reformation that is essential for any recovery to be likely throughout this nation, one which has given the world the most hope for fair and just governance and a collective optimism that was so unique in all human history. This final reform involves our individual or personal misbehaviors. It, unlike the reforms discussed previous to this, MUST begin immediately.

To put a stop to this unraveling process that Greg and I have witnessed in governmental, fiscal and individual behaviors, certain truths must be recognized. All of us need to have the same higher and nobler vision. It has come to a woeful state of affairs that it takes a child and a dog to recommend these needed changes. They must come from all of you as well. And to assist in beginning this process, please take further time away from your daily pursuits and study the last reform act. (see Appendix: **Individual Behavior Reform Act of 2012**). After your doing so, I will only have a few short observations to make, and the course and very survival of your nation will be in your hands.

FOURTEEN: THE VERY FINAL EPILOGUE

So there you have it. I told you at the outset that what I had to report was both disturbing and tragic. It seems to have been an ongoing pattern since the loss of Wally's and my family in Atlantic City. Now, as you know, I've lost the last surviving member of my extended family. Plus, the loss of my rescuers that awful day our parents were murdered only adds to my overwhelming loneliness. In such a short time all of us were a part of something so transforming and yet, now it is on the verge of dissolution and paralysis. Something so trivial-sounding as "behavior" can have such a sweeping national, even international, impact.

But I have kept my promise to tell you everything that has happened to us Wagoners since that day we appeared at the United Nations Assembly. Between what Greg and Lilyanne have so faithfully reported to me and my own observations and comments, you have now read or been told the full extent of our travels and transformations.

The loss of my little brother and dearest companions, Flo and Greg, has left a gulf in me that will never be filled. And the real potential for this nation, one that has been forged with such courage, hopes and tragic loss of life in wars and social strife, to fully develop and be the beacon it was meant to be to all this world and any others that may one day venture here, is on the very edge of disintegrating. Greg's vision was not just imaginary; it was prophetic to the core. Wisdom, wonder and willingness of all to sacrifice and discipline themselves are the keys to whatever future this land... and world... will have.

But before I conclude this testament, I need to describe briefly what happened and was said the last day that I had the privilege of being with all the remaining Wagoners and Shrivers. After this day, Rita and Jennifer departed to launch a search, that to my knowledge has never uncovered exactly who did it and why my brother, Flo and Greg were so brutally killed. I understand their search is spreading over the entire country, as they enlist more and more allies from their days of organizing the communities here in the Puget Sound.

And both Stella and Phil Shriver have returned to their new home in one of the newly established communities in eastern King County. He has been given command again of another Coast Guard vessel. And Happy has rejoined him in this assignment.

Only Sophie, Frank and their kids' families have stayed with me or vise versa. I intend to set aside any of my Herald powers that may remain. Once I have finished saying what I conveyed to Sophie one day as we sat by the shoreline on the lake behind the Quinault Lodge, I will retire from those duties. The Wagoners, as they once existed and were commissioned by my grandfather, Walt, will be history. Who really knows whether anyone will remember or care that we ever existed? My guess is that given the work ahead for this country... few will. But it is on that note that I want and need to complete my final observations and suggestions for the individual behavior lapses that have mounted so dangerously throughout this land.

The head-long fall over the precipice into chaos and radical division may have already occurred. The staggering tragedy that occurred on that awful July 29th afternoon may have exposed forever the weaknesses and handicaps that this nation cannot overcome. Or maybe there is imbedded in each surviving individual a desire to become better, fight for goodness and mercy and work unceasingly to do what is right. That would be the best legacy possible for my brother, Flo and my dearest friend, Greg. Please... do better... all of you. There will be no second chances after this.

So what follows now is what I discussed with Sophie that afternoon, about two months after the death of my brother and our dearest companions. Sophie was so patient with me, as I droned on and on. She then offered to have Frank type and collate all this material and make sure it gets into the proper hands for the appropriate dissemination. Here are my last comments for any public review and consideration.

First off, these earthquakes and tsunamis were classic examples of the indifference of the cosmos or our home planet... Earth... to life. Galaxies form, disperse, gravitate toward one another, collide and disappear. The silence of the void of space cries out for some kind of balance for this stark indifference to the beauty of life and rebirth.

But there is a balancing force, if you will. All the physical laws of the Universe indicate there is a balance, something equal and opposite that counteracts galactic movements, events... even indifference. Evil deeds are countered by heroic ones. Colliding stars and planets are balanced by the creation of new ones. And, dear ones, what Walt, Wally and my dearest companions that are now departed have impressed on me is that there is a Holy One who cares, Who inspires and gives hope, Who urges a sense of wonder, a quest for wisdom and a willingness to sacrifice and discipline ourselves for the sake of life now and for the one that follows after our passing. Indifference is met by the Holy, and we are not abandoned or alone. We are sheltered from this indifference. We are blessed.

Next, I need to fill you in on what I sense is the final magical action of Wally, and probably at Walt's urging: his choosing certain children to reside in the newly established communities here in the westernmost portion of the country. It was their final gift to us all. These children will become the beacons for this weary land. They are to become this country's finest artists, scientists, social and political leaders, parents and citizens. In them will reside the best examples of behavior... in whatever they do. They will become our guides on the long road of recovery ahead.

In addition, I need to say that you now have been given the final key of what we Wagoners have tried to demonstrate, say and perform again and again. It can be simply summed up by the phrase: "starting over". It's what we have to do, whether after a disaster, a tragedy, a mistake or a lapse in judgment and its resulting bad behavior. You, I, everyone must go on, keep going on, keep starting over. It takes courage and will power, but you must do it.

And of course, there is the issue of Greg's vision of

168

our becoming the "Disunited States of America". Is that inevitable? Can it be avoided? Can we rediscover our collective souls and work together to become wise, think, be innovative and act in concert with one another? Only if we can, will we stay United. And if we don't, so much of what we Wagoners have done and suffered will have been in vain.

And as I approach the very end of my "to do" list, I want to provide you with an old-time list of rules that were often posted in dairy barns throughout this land. As simple as they are, they seem to give a direction for the hard work that is ahead for all of us. Remember: there is to be no more magic. What's left now are hard choices and hard work. Let the "Barn Rules" help guide you (see Appendix: **Barn Rules**).

This brings me to one of the last things I have to say. And sadly, it reaches down to the very core of my being; it's that I couldn't do enough to save my brother or my closest friends. Like someone desperately struggling to save someone from dying and having him clutching frantically onto you, begging you to help, as he turned progressively bluer and bluer with foam beginning to ooze out the sides of his mouth. Despite all you attempt, he finally gasps and goes limp. His dying and death; his cries and struggle... all haunt you for the rest of your life.

You couldn't do enough... I couldn't do enough. All the magic that we performed throughout this land and world wasn't enough to save Wally, Flo and Greg. And now we are facing momentous struggles throughout this land and elsewhere.

EVERYONE!
LISTEN TO ME!!!
DO ALL YOU CAN!

BE THE BEST YOU CAN BE!
AND JUST MAYBE... **MAYBE** ... IT WILL BE
ENOUGH TO RESET OUR NATION'S
COMPASS.

.

****

And, finally, my hope for each of you can be best described by the following.

Somewhere there reside the mortal remains of my brother and my two dearest friends. There can be no doubt that by now each has long been buried under mounds of leaves, drifting snow and shifting pine needles. Their gravesites, unlike those at the entrance to the Arlington National Cemetery, will forever be unsung and unknown.

But each site is now and always shall be blessed with that most hallowed of remembrances and most comforting of prayers: "Known Only to God". There can be no more noble a tribute, nor a more reassuring benediction. For each of them, I know that this will be enough.

And ultimately, for each of you hero's out there, at the end of your individual journeys, being known only to God could be your final recognition; find comfort and peace in that. Above and despite all else, this surely is enough.

APPENDIX

1. Rialto Beach:

2. Lake Quinault Lodge:

---

[2] Image used courtesy of Olympic National Park, Lake Quinault, Washington.

3. Cascadian Fault:

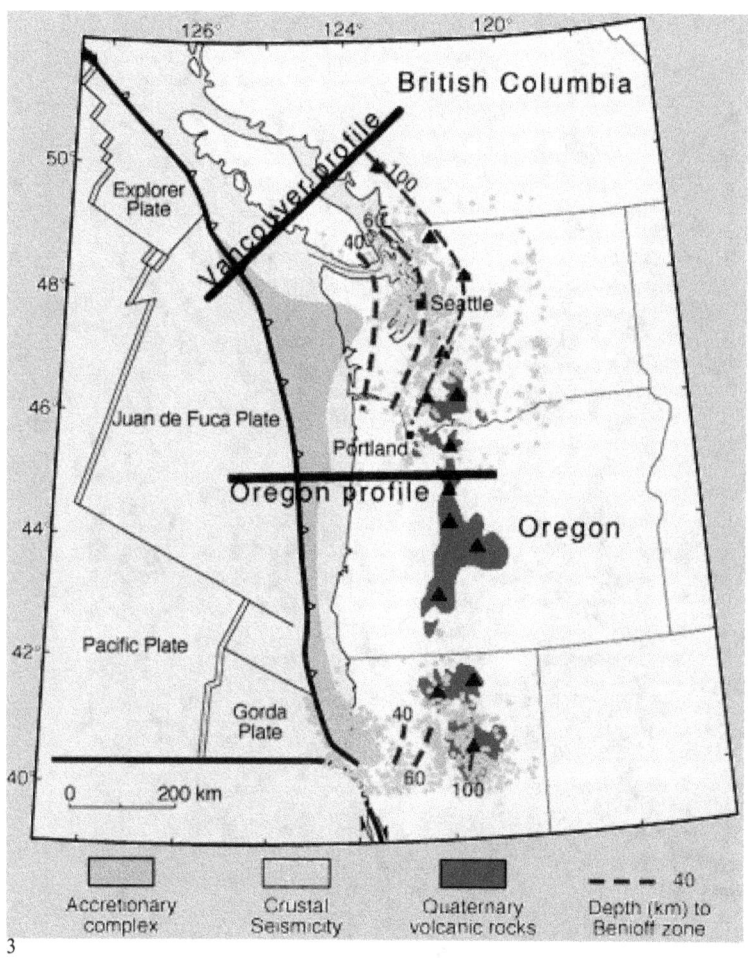

3 Image used courtesy of USGS, "Cascadia Subduction Zone".

4. San Andreas Fault:

---

[4] Sanandreas.jpg Wikipedia Commons. Source:USGS, www.nationalatlas.gov.

5. Cascade Eruptions During the Past 4,000 Years:

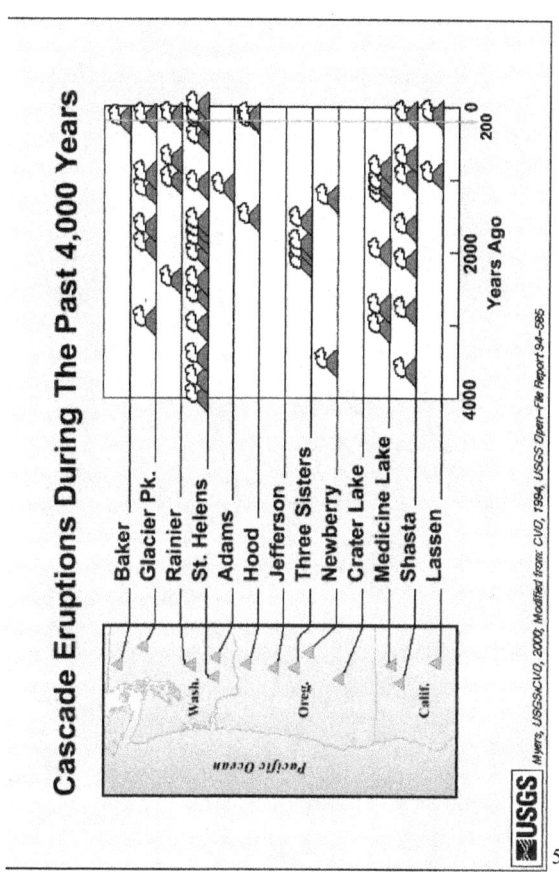

[5] Image used courtesy of USGS, "Cascadia eruptions in the last 4000 Years".

6. Earth's Tectonic Plates:

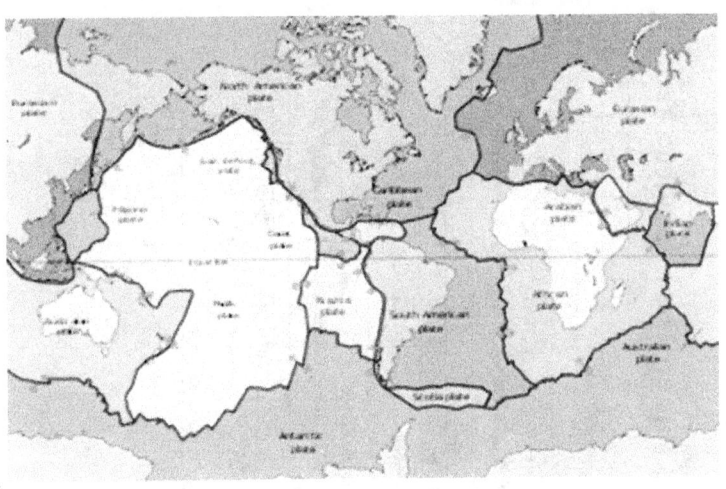

6

[6]Plates tect2 en.svg from Wikipedia Commons. Source: USGS, http://usgs.gov.

7. The Sacramento River:

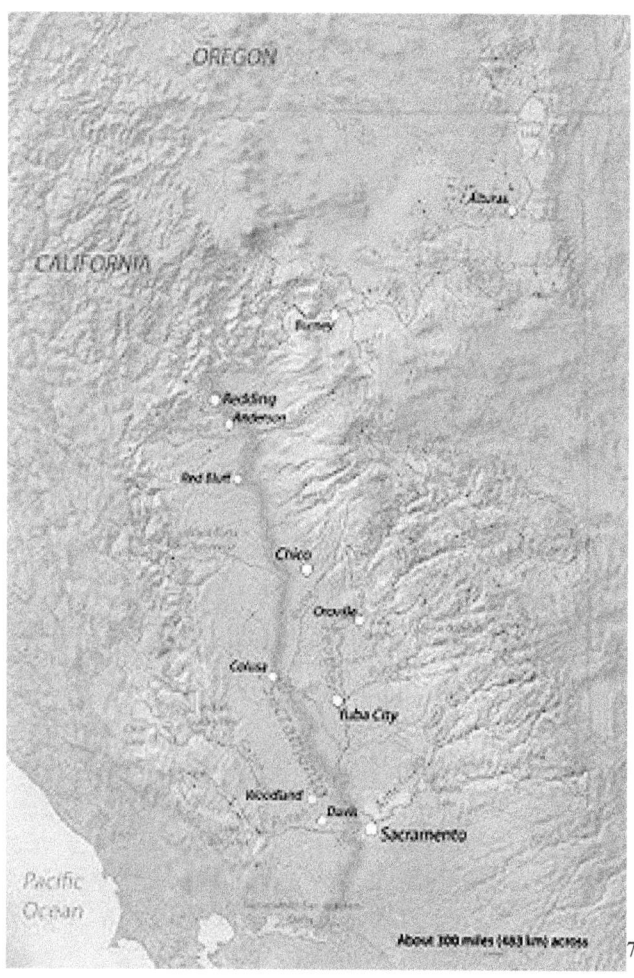

---

8. The Disunited States of America:

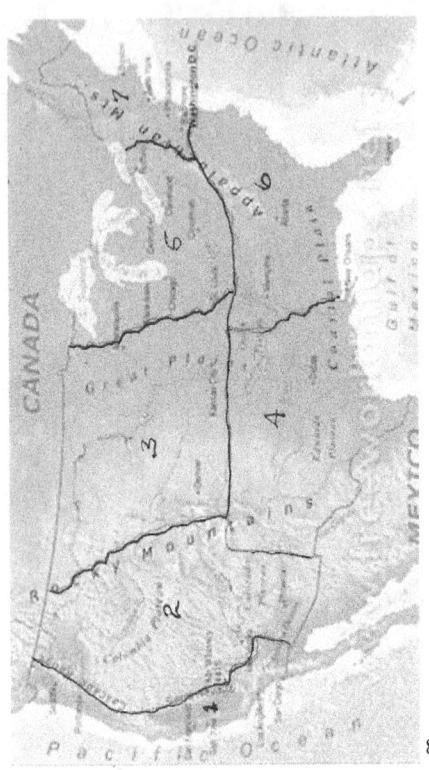

8 Image courtesy of www.freeworldmaps.net.

1. The Sovereign State of Pacifica
2. The Sovereign State of Cascadia
3. The Sovereign State of Missoura
4. The Sovereign State of Texahoma
5. The Sovereign State of Lincoln
6. The Sovereign State of Appalachia
7. The Sovereign State of Katadan

9. Congressional Reform Act of 2012:

 1. Term Limits: (*everything in parentheses and italicized is my own addition to this document... Bernie, the Wagoner's Herald*)
 12 years only, using one of the possible options below. (*note: Just as there are term limits to the Presidency, so there should be such for Congress and the Supreme Court. None of the Founding Fathers could have anticipated how gerrymandering, the advent of chronic, regional, non-representative election after election, the mesmerizing effect of earmarks or the development of Congressional members self-interest rising above the general good for all Americans would keep members continually reelected far beyond their useful and productive tenure.*)
> A. Two, Six-year Senate terms.
> B. Six, Two-year House terms.
> C. One, Six-year Senate term and three, Two-year House terms.This applies to all Senate and Congressional Aides as well.

 2. No Tenure/ No pension:
 A Congressman collects a salary while in office and receives no pay when he or she is out of office. (*Limiting the time each Congressman/woman serves to 12 years will automatically disqualify anyone from reaching the 20 years of service required for receiving their now, lucrative pensions.*)

 3. Congress will continue to purchase their own retirement plan, just as all Americans do. (*It will be rolled over once they leave office into whatever retirement plan they choose, once they rejoin the civilian workforce.*)

4. Congress will no longer vote for a pay raise for themselves, (*or for the President or any Supreme Court members for the present or for any future timeframe. All three branches of governments' pay will rise by the lower of CPI or 3% , provided it is approved every two years by a standard, nationwide proposition during each national election. The people are to regain   control of when, for how long and how much compensation their representatives are to receive for those who represent them, and for how much they are to be paid to do so*).

5. Congress loses their current health care system and participates in the same health care system as the American people. (*They are free to join any of the standard health care plans available to any other citizen offered within the geographical region they serve. They cannot have a 'Cadillac Plan', while the rest of the country's citizens scramble to get whatever coverage they can. If there is rationing of care, Congress, the President and the Supreme Court members must share in that process. It's a matter of fairness and good leadership.*)

6. Congress must equally abide by all laws they pass. (*Which shall include living within their means, both personally and by the laws they pass. It shall become a law that government shall have a balanced budget and passed at a given time or the Congressmen/women will be fined for any delay or overages.*)

7. Lobbying Congress will be illegal; and if committed by a former Senator or member of the House of Representative, it will be considered a felony. (*This activity has become a burden on every Congressman/women's time and is too large a temptation to not feel obligated to generous donors, who are often*

scattered amongst various lobbyists. The taint and distraction of this activity needs to be removed.)[9]

---

[9] Used with the knowledge of and adapted from "Congressional Reform Act of 2010", Petition Author, Care2 petition site, Care2.com. And first introduced to the author by K.V. Easterwood.

10. The Constitution of the United States of America:
(abridged without the inclusion of Amendments)

WE THE PEOPLE of the United States, in Order to form a more perfect Union, establish Justice, provide for the common defense, promote the general Welfare, and secure the Blessings of Liberty to ourselves and our Posterity, do ordain and establish this Constitution for the United States of America.

Article I

Section 1: All legislative Powers herein granted shall be vested in a Congress of the United States, which shall consist of a Senate and House of Representatives.

Section 2: The House of Representatives shall be composed of Members chosen every second Year by the People of the several states, and the Electors in each State shall have the Qualifications requisite for Electors of the most numerous Branch of the State Legislature.

Section 3: The Senate of the United States shall be composed of two Senators from each State, chosen by the legislature thereof for six Years; and each Senator shall have one vote.

Section 4: The Times, Places and Manner of holding Elections for Senators and Representatives, shall be prescribed in each State by the Legislature thereof; but the Congress may at any time by Law make or alter such Regulations, except as to the Places of choosing Senators.

Section 5: Each House shall be the Judge of the Elections, Returns and Qualifications of its own Members, and a Majority of each shall constitute a Quorum to do Business; but a smaller Number may adjourn from day to day, and may be authorized to compel the Attendance of absent

Members, in such Manner, and under such Penalties as each House may provide.

Section 6: The Senators and Representatives shall receive a Compensation for their Services, to be ascertained by Law, and paid out of the Treasury of the United States. They shall in all Cases, except Treason, Felony and Breach of the Peace, be privileged from Arrest during their Attendance at the Session of their respective Houses, and in going to and returning from the same; and for any Speech or Debate in either House, they shall not be questioned in any other Place.

Section 7: All Bills for raising Revenue shall originate in the House of Representatives; but the Senate may propose or concur with Amendments as on other Bills.

Section 8: The Congress shall have Power To lay and collect Taxes, Duties, Imposts and Excises, to pay the Debt and provide for the common Defense and general Welfare of the United States; and all Duties, Imposts and Excises shall be uniform throughout the United States;

To borrow Money on the credit of the United States;

To regulate Commerce with foreign Nations, and among the several States, and with the Indian Tribes;

To establish a uniform Rule of Naturalization, and uniform Laws on the subject of Bankruptcies throughout the United States;

To coin Money, regulate the Value thereof, and of foreign Coin, and fix the Standard of Weights and Measures;

To provide for the Punishment of counterfeiting the Securities and current Coin of the United States;

To establish Post Offices and post Roads;

To promote the Progress of Science and useful Arts, by securing for limited Times to Authors and Inventors the exclusive Right to their respective Writings and

Discoveries;

To constitute Tribunals inferior to the Supreme Court;

To define and punish Piracies and Felonies committed on the high Seas, and Offenses against the Law of Nations;

To declare War, grant Letters of Marque and Reprisal, and make Rules concerning Captures on Land and Water;

To raise and support Armies, but *Appropriation of Money to that Use shall be no longer Term than two Years;* (italics and underline Bernie's doing)

To provide and maintain a Navy;

To make Rules for the Government and Regulation of the land and naval Forces;

To provide for calling forth the Militia to execute the Laws of the Union, suppress Insurrections and repel Invasions;

To provide for organizing, arming and discipline, the Militia, and for governing such part of them as may be employed in the Service of the United States...;

To exercise exclusive Legislation in all Cases whatsoever, ...;

To make all Laws which shall be necessary and proper for carrying into Execution the foregoing Powers, and all other Powers vested by this Constitution in the Government of the United States.... .

Section 9: The Migration or Importation of such Persons as any of the States now existing shall think proper to admit, shall be prohibited by the Congress prior to the Year one thousand eight hundred and eight, but a Tax or duty may be imposed on such Importation, not exceeding ten dollars for each person.

The Privilege of the Writ of Habeas Corpus shall not be suspended, unless when in Cases of Rebellion or Invasion the public Safety may require it.

No Bill of Attainder or ex post facto Law shall be passed.

No capitation, or other direct, Tax shall be laid, unless in Proportion to the Census or enumeration herein before directed to be taken.

No Tax or Duty shall be laid on Articles exported from any State.

No Preference shall be given by any Regulation of Commerce or Revenue to the Ports of one State over those of another; nor shall Vessels bout to, or from, one State, be obliged to enter, clear or pay Duties in another.

No Money shall be drawn from the Treasury, but in Consequence of Appropriations made by Law; and a regular Statement and Account of the Receipts and Expenditures of all public Money shall be published from time to time.

No Title of Nobility shall be granted by the United States: and no Person holding any Office of Profit or Trust under them, shall, without the Consent of the Congress, accept of any present, Emolument, Office, or Title, of any kind whatever, from any King, Prince, or foreign State.

Section 10. No State shall enter into any Treaty, Alliance or Confederation; grant Letters of Marque and Reprisal; coin Money; emit Bills of Credit; make any Thing but gold and silver Coin a Tender in Payment of Debts; pass any Bill of Attainder, ex post facto Law, or grant any Title of Nobility.

No State shall, without the Consent of the Congress, lay any Imposts or Duties on Imports or Exports, except what may be absolutely necessary for executing it's inspection Laws: and the net Produce of all Duties and Imports, laid by any State on Imports or Exports, shall be for the Use of the Treasury of the United States; and all such Laws shall be subject to the Revision and Control of Congress.

No State shall, without the Consent of Congress, lay any Duty of Tonnage, keep Troops, or Ships of War in time of Peace, enter into any Agreement of Compact with another State, or with a foreign Power, or engage in War, unless actually invaded, or in such imminent Danger as will not admit of delay.

Article II

Section 1. The executive Power shall be vested in a President of the United States of America. He shall hold his Office during the Term of four Years, and, together with the Vice President, chosen for the same Term, be elected, as follows:

Each State shall appoint, in such Manner as the Legislature thereof may direct, a Number of Electors, equal to the whole Number of Senators and Representatives to which the State may be entitled in the Congress; but no Senator or Representative, or Person holding an Office of Trust or Profit under the United States, shall be appointed an Elector.

The Electors shall meet in their respective States, and vote by Ballot for two Persons, of whom one at least shall not be an Inhabitant of the same State with themselves. And they shall make a List of all the Persons voted for, and of the Number of Votes for each; which List they shall sign and certify, and transmit sealed to the Seat of the Government of the United States, directed to the President of the Senate. The President of the Senate shall, in the Presence of the Senate and House of Representatives, open all the Certificates, and the Votes shall then be counted. The Person having the greatest Number of Votes shall be the President, if such Number be a Majority of the whole Number of Electors appointed; and if there be more than one who have such Majority, and have an equal Number of Votes, then the House of Representatives shall immediately chuse by Ballot one of them for President; and if no Person have a Majority, then from the five highest of the List the said House shall in like manner chuse the President. But in chusing the President, the Votes shall be taken by States, the Representative from each State having one Vote; A quorum for this purpose shall consist of a Member or Members from two thirds of the States, and a Majority of all the States shall be necessary to a Choice. In every Case, after the Choice of the President, the Person having the greatest Number of Votes of the Electors shall be the Vice President. But if there should remain two or more who have equal Votes, the Senate shall chuse from them by Ballot the Vice President.

The Congress may determine the Time of chusing the Electors, and the Day on which they shall give their Votes; which Day shall be the same throughout the United States.

No Person except a natural born Citizen, or a Citizen of the United States, at the time of the Adoption of this Constitution, shall be eligible to the Office of President; neither shall any Person be eligible to that Office who shall not have attained to the Age of thirty five Years, and been fourteen Years a Resident within the United States.

In Case of the Removal of the President from Office, or of his Death, Resignation, or Inability to discharge the Powers and Duties of the said Office, the Same shall devolve on the Vice President, and the Congress may by Law provide for the Case of Removal, Death, Resignation or Inability, both the President and Vice President, declaring what Officer shall then act as President, and such Officer shall act accordingly, until the Disability be removed, or a President shall be elected.

The President shall, at states Times, receive for his Services, a Compensation, which shall neither be increased nor diminished during the Period for which he shall have been elected, and he shall not receive within that Period any other Emolument from the United States, or any of them.

Before he enter on the Execution of his Office, he shall take the following Oath or Affirmation:--"I do solemnly swear (or affirm) that I will faithfully execute the Office of President of the United States, and will to the best of my Ability, preserve, protect and defend the Constitution of the Unites States."

Section 2. The President shall be Commander in Chief of the Army and Navy of the United States, and of the Militia of the several States, when called into the actual Service of the United States; he may require the Opinion, in writing, of the principal Officer in each of the executive Departments, upon any Subject relating to the Duties of their respective Offices, and he shall have Power to grant Reprieves and Pardons for Offenses against the United States, except in Cases of Impeachment.

He shall have Power, by and with the Advice and Consent of the Senate, to make Treaties, provided two thirds of the Senators present concur; and he shall nominate, and by and with the Advice and Consent of the Senate, shall appoint Ambassadors, other public Ministers and Consuls, Judges of the supreme Court, and all other Officer of the United States, whose Appointments are not herein otherwise provided for, and which shall be established by Law: but the Congress may by Law vest the Appointment of such inferior Officers, as they think proper, in the President alone, in the Courts of Law, or in the Heads of Departments.

The President shall have Power to fill up all Vacancies that may happen during the Recess of the Senate, by granting Commissions which shall expire at the End of their next Session.

Section 3. He shall from time to time give to the Congress Information of the State of the Union, and recommend to their Consideration such Measures as he shall judge necessary and expedient; he may, on extraordinary Occasions, convene both Houses, or either of them, and in Case of Disagreement between them, with Respect to the Time of Adjournment, he may adjourn them to such Time as he shall think proper; he shall receive Ambassadors and other public Ministers; he shall take Care that the Laws be faithfully executed, and shall Commission all the Officer of the United States.

Section 4. The President, Vice President and all civil Officer of the United States, shall be removed from Office on Impeachment for, and Conviction of, Treason, Bribery, or other high Crimes and Misdemeanors.

Article III

Section 1. The judicial Power of the United States shall be vested in one supreme Court, and in such inferior Courts as the Congress may from time to time ordain and establish. The Judges, both of the supreme and inferior Courts, shall hold their offices during good Behaviour, and shall, at stated times, receive for their Services a Compensation, which shall not be diminished during their continuance in Office.

Section 2. The judicial Power shall extend to all Cases, in Law and Equity, arising under this Constitution, the Laws of the United States, and Treaties made, or which shall be made, under their Authority; -- to all Cases affecting Ambassadors, other publish Ministers and Consuls....

Section 3. Treason against the United States, shall consist only in levying War against them, or in adhering to their Enemies, given them Aid and Comfort. No Person shall be convicted of Treason unless on the Testimony of two Witnesses to the same overt Act, or on Confession in open Court. The Congress shall have Power to declare the Punishment of Treason, but no Attainder of Treason shall work Corruption of Blood, or Forfeiture except during Life of the Person attained.

Article IV

Section 1. Full Faith and Credit shall be given in each State to the public Acts, Records, and judicial Proceedings of every other State. And the Congress may by general Laws prescribe the Manner in which such Acts, Records and Proceedings shall be proved, and the Effect thereof.

Section 2. The Citizens of each State shall be entitled to all Privileges and Immunities of Citizens in the several States.

A Person charged in any State with Treason, Felony, or other Crime, who shall flee from Justice, and be found in another State, shall on Demand of the executive Authority of the State from which he fled, be delivered up, to be removed to the State having Jurisdiction of the Crime.

No person held to Service or Labour in one State, under the Laws thereof, escaping into another, shall, in Consequence of any Law or Regulation therein, be discharged from such Service or Labour, but shall be delivered up on Claim of the Party to whom such Service or Labour may be due.

Section 3. New States may be admitted by the Congress

into this Union; but no new State shall be formed or erected within the Jurisdiction of any other State; nor any State be formed by the Junction of two or more States, or Parts of States, without the Consent of the Legislatures of the States concerned as well as of the Congress.

The Congress shall have Power to dispose of and make all needful Rules and Regulations respecting the Territory or other Property belonging to the United States; and nothing in this Constitution shall be so construed as to Prejudice any Claims of the United States, or of any particular State.

Section 4. The United States shall guarantee to every State in this Union a Republican Form of Government, and shall protect each of them against Invasion; and on Application of the Legislature, or of the Executive (when the Legislature cannot be convened), against domestic Violence.

Article V

The Congress, whenever two thirds of both Houses shall deem it necessary, shall propose Amendments to this Constitution, or, on the Application of the Legislatures of two thirds of the several States, shall call a Convention for proposing Amendments, which, in either Case, shall be valid to all Intents and Purposes, as Part of this Constitution, when ratified by the Legislatures of three fourths of the several States, or by Conventions in three fourths thereof, as the one or the other Mode of Ratification may be proposed by the Congress; Provided that no Amendment which may be made prior to the Year One thousand eight hundred and eight shall in any Manner affect the first and fourth Clauses in the Ninth Section of the first Article; and that no State, without its Consent, shall be deprived of its equal Suffrage in the Senate.

Article VI

All debts contracted and Engagements entered into, before the Adoption of this Constitution, shall be as valid against the United States under this Constitution, as under the Confederation.

This Constitution, and the Laws of the United States which shall be made in Pursuance thereof; and all Treaties made, or which shall be made, under the Authority of the United States, shall be the supreme Law of the Land; and the Judges in every State shall be bound thereby, and Thing in the Constitution or Laws of any State to the Contrary notwithstanding.

The Senators and Representatives before mentioned, and the Members of the several State Legislatures, and all executive and judicial Officers, both of the United States and of the several States, shall be bound by Oath or Affirmation, to support this Constitution; but no religious Test shall ever be required as a Qualification to any Office or public Trust under the United States.

Article VII

The Ratification of the Conventions of nine States, shall be sufficient for the Establishment of this Constitution between the States so ratifying the Same.

The Word, "the", being interlined between the seventh and eight Line of the first Page, the Word "Thirty" being partly written on an Erazure in the fifteenth Line of the first Page, The Words "is tried" being interlined between the thirty second and thirty third Lines of the first Page and the Word "the" being interlined between the forty third and forty fourth Lines of the second Page.

Attest William Jackson Secretary

Done in Convention by the Unanimous Consent of the States present the Seventeenth Day of September in the year of our Lord one thousand seven hundred and Eighty seven and of the Independence of the United States of America the Twelfth in witness whereof We have hereunto subscribed our Names,

George Washington- President.....[10]

---

[10] Used with permission in its original form from the American Civil Liberties Union, as printed and distributed in their own publication on an ongoing basis on October 1, 2010.

11. Voting Reform Act of 2012:

1. You must read or understand English.
2. You must vote only in a certified voting location; on a paper ballot, written in English.
3. There are to be no absentee or mail-in ballots, unless you are certified by a physician as being unable to travel safely or easily to a voting center. But even then, you will have to pass the written test which would be given orally over the telephone. (See below)
4. Military personnel will also be provided the appropriate voting centers and all returns everywhere are to be left uncounted until their ballots are returned to the mainland USA.
5. Every voter must pass a test given in English in your respective voting center. The contents of which will not be known until the time You vote. There will be different tests, similar to the driver's license exams, to avoid most cheating. Once you pass the test regarding the Constitution, candidates and any propositions, you can then vote.
6. No one is to pay you, give you a meal or special favors to buy or curry your vote. You are to report any such activity immediately. And you forfeit your right to vote if you accept anything of this nature.
7. Finally, it is to become the law that you vote. If you don't, there will be severe fines imposed.

12. Financial Reform Act of 2012:

1. Begin deleveraging as soon as possible; in other
   words reduce debt of any borrowing that is
   unsustainable, whether the debt is on a
   national, state, local or individual level.
   Do so by:
   -Increasing manufacturing within the
   country, reversing the economic
   disaster caused by massive off-shoring of
   the nation's industrial base.
   - Increasing exports.
   - Reduce as humanly as possible the
   spending on social contracts, e.g. social
   security, Medicare, food stamps, income
   supplements. As painful as this step will be,
   it has to be done. Over population of the
   country has created an economic
   whirlpool, sucking the life's blood out of the
   economy. Entitlements will now have to be
   asset tested to determine the greatest need.
   There will be no more universal entitlements
   possible. Human rights, such as universal
   medical care, social network assistance and
   government pensions, which decades ago
   became popular and were so humanely
   funded, can no longer be afforded without
   an individual meeting certain qualifications.
   National, State and local bankruptcy is
   just around the corner if the policies now in
   force continue as is. The natural rights of
   life, liberty and the pursuit of happiness
   have to be guaranteed and ever-protected.

But the list of other rights will unfortunately become limited to only the neediest.

-Change the taxation model (See below for details).

-Balance the national budget and begin to significantly pay down the nation's debt.

-Let modest deflation reduce some of the unsustainable cost of goods and services. Allow for no more than a ten percent drop in prices over the next four years.

-Institute a devaluation of all goods, services, wages and housing. To do this, there will be an additional Index added to the already monthly CPI or Consumer Price Index, where the federal government calculates the rise or fall of the costs of goods and services. Within this next year the new Index, the Consumer Assessment Index, will begin determining what devaluation of goods, services, wages and housing will be instituted and on what date it will happen. To start with there will be an annual 10% devaluation, and by the end of four years there will be a 50% total devaluation of all these categories. Couple that with the lowering of values due to deflation during this same period of 10%, and there will be a total devaluation of 60%, combining both passive and active methods apart from and through this new commission.

By the end of this time period the cost of a

present home of $120,000.00 will then be $48,000.00: a 60% loss in value. And at the same time the now, average annual wage of someone in this country of $40,000.00 will become $16,000.00. And the mortgage cost of this now $48,000 home will be $295.54 per month on a 30 year, 5% fixed loan. It will only be $215.54 per month on a 30 year, 3.5% fixed loan. And if the wage earner making $16,000 per year then makes $1,333 per month, this mortgage payment will only be 18.5% of his monthly income. Plus, keep in mind that by the end of this same four years, taxes in this country will then be based on consumption, not income. The more this individual saves, the less will be his or her tax obligation.

2. Change the taxation model from income to a combination of consumption taxation:

 - A VAT or Value Added Tax is one in which a tax is collected on the "value added" to a product, material or service at each stage of its being manufactured or distributed or performed. There most likely will be exceptions to this tax, such as basic food stuffs and medicine. And there would likely be an income threshold, below which there would be some kind of rebate. This form of taxation is presently being used in many countries throughout the world. It would be pegged at a 20% level when this method of taxation would be initiated within this next year.

-A SSCT or Savings Stimulus consumption tax would be also be instituted by the end of this same four year period. It will serve to encourage saving and investment. It will be determined by the difference between the worker's annual wage and the amount he or she saved or invested. The more saved, the less taxed. It will be a 10% tax and one that is distributed at first to the federal government, but eventually will only be Used by the various states and local governments.

-An Energy Tax of 10% will also be Collected on the use of gasoline, coal, natural gas and electricity. Half of the money's collected through this form of taxation will go towards developing and erecting new, carbon-free forms of energy.

3. Formation of manufacturing and small business cooperatives:

-By uniting in a loose federation such a cooperative, the manufacturing of appliances, other consumer goods and the suppliers and refiners of basic materials such as iron, aluminum, silver or other precious metals, which have been off-shored over the last two or three decades, can begin to be returned to the mainland.

-By a cooperative's charter, there is a one worker, one vote mandate, so unionization is not necessary. It is democratically organized and operated. Certain tax incentives and investment benefits will be given for the organization of cooperatives. They will not be meant to supplant individual entrepreneurs or to stifle competition and quality workmanship. But its purpose is to bring back the manufacturing base to this country and to do so will require both creative and cooperative ventures.

4. A new economic foundation must replace the current one that does not give nearly enough respect for and recognition of the need for building on the need to recognize the misbehaviors and day-to-day behaviors of each of us. There have to be government regulations, which will provide oversight to any developing misbehaviors. And there has to be incorporated into the revision of our nation's economy the time-tested, but under recognized, values of fairness, confidence and the ongoing narrative throughout human history of whether these two bench marks are being adequately met.[11]

---

[11] Major portions of this section are only possible with the help and guidance from S.D. Price.

13. Individual Behavior Reform Act of 2012:

1. The governed... each of us... must be willing;
   the governing... each of them... must be
   able, humble and driven to perform ongoing
   self-examinations as to their motives,
   actions and decisions.
2. We must all seek the "common" good; that
   which is held universally possible,
   reasonable and affordable, given the limits
   of our abilities and resources. We cannot
   achieve the "perfect" or "ultimate" good.
   The limitations within each of us, physically,
   emotionally and spiritually prevent that. But
   the common good is one that will provide us
   each an opportunity to attain and maintain
   good behavior... each and every one of us.
   And to achieve this, the following guidelines
   are necessary for each of us:
   -Keep your life's goals, needs and
   expectations SIMPLE.
   -Don't avoid hard decisions... expect them.
   But within each of us is the capacity to be
   wise and creative.
   -Dare to love, to be steadfastly loyal, to
   hope, to remain ever-aware, to take risks, to
   serve others and to laugh at yourself and at
   this remarkable adventure called life.
   Each of you can become heroes. Just dare
   yourself to be so.
   -Avoid bluster, bravado, a sense of your
   own self-importance. Each of us is of value,
   but not so much that it overrides that of

others around us.

-Pray unceasingly to seek and experience the Holy: the only indwelling Presence and Power that will counterbalance the cosmic indifference, overcome the unspeakable evil and prevent us from succumbing to the tantalizing corruption which can envelope us all... at any moment.[12]

---

[12] And obvious credit has to be given here to the years this author has spent listening to and being influenced by The Wagoners and Greg.

14. Barn Rules:

"If you unlock it, lock it back.
If you open it, close it.
If you borrow it, return it.
If you don't know, ask.
If you drive it, check the oil.
If you lose it, replace it.
If it doesn't concern you, don't mess with it.
If you turn it on, turn it off.
If you break it, fix it.
If you move it, put it back.
If you throw it down, pick it up.
If you ride it, feed it.
If it drinks water, give it some.
And if you fall off, get back on."[13]

….. Begin anew.
Start over.
Never… ever … stop trying.
Again and again and again.

---

[13] From an image reprinted and pasted in "Country" magazine,
June/July 2004 issue, on page 5. Used with their knowledge. Original
author of "Barn Rules" is unknown.

REFERENCES

1. <u>Major American Writers, 3rd Edition, Volume 2</u>, edited by Howard Mumford Jones, Ernest E. Leisy, Richard M. Ludwig. Harcourt, Brace and Co., New York, 1952.

2. <u>Rescuing a Broken America - Why America is Deeply Divided and How to Heal it Constitutionally</u>, Michael Coffman. Morgan James Publishing, Garden City, New York, 2010.

3. <u>Animal Spirits-How Human Psychology Drives the Economy, and Why it Matters for Global Capitalism</u>, George A.Akerlof and Robert J. Shiller. Princeton University Press, Princeton, New Jersey, 2009.

4. <u>Wikipedia, The Free Encyclopedica</u>: Behavior, List of Cognitive Biases, Value Added Tax, GDP vs GPI, Consumption Tax, Deleverage

5. <u>The Lucifer Effect: Understanding How Good People Turn Evil</u>, Philip Zimbardo. Random House, New York, 2007.

6. <u>Human Behavior and the Social Environment - Macro Level: Groups, Communities and Organizations</u>, Katherine van Wormer, Fred H. Besthorn, Thomas Keefe. Oxford University Press, New York, 2007.

7. <u>Dimensions of Human Behavior - Person and Environment</u>, Elizabeth D. Hutchison. Sage Publications, Thousand Oaks, Calif., 2003.

8. <u>Dimensions of Human Behavior - The Changing Life Course</u>, Elizabeth D. Hutchison. Sage Publications, Thousand Oaks, Calif., 2003.

9. <u>Guyland - The Perilous World Where Boys Become</u>

<u>Men</u>, Michael Kimmel. Harper Collins, New York, 2008.

10. <u>On Whitman</u>, Thomas C.K. Williams. Princeton University Press, Princeton, New Jersey, 2010.

11. <u>The Broken Branch: How Congress is Failing America and How to Get it Back on Track</u>, Thomas E. Mann and Norman J. Ornstein. Oxford University Press, New York, 2006.

12. <u>Nemesis - The Last Days of the American Republic</u>, Chalmers Johnson. Metropolitan Books, Henry Holt and Co., New York, 2006.

13. <u>The Constitution of the United States of America</u>. American Civil Liberties Union, New York.